A TRAGIC ACT

A CHARLETON HOUSE MYSTERY

KATE P ADAMS

All characters in this publication, other than those clearly in the public domain, are fictitious and any resemblance to real people, alive or dead, is purely coincidental.

Paperback ISBN 978-1-7335619-7-6

Cover design by Dar Albert

ALSO BY KATE P ADAMS

Death by Dark Roast

A Killer Wedding

Sleep Like the Dead

A Deadly Ride

Mulled Wine and Murder

A Tragic Act

To

Gwen Thomson

Thank you for all the laughter on our many theatrical adventures

CHAPTER 1

'I considered a career on the stage, I had quite a lot of offers. I was even asked to play Juliet,' said Joyce proudly.

'So you met Shakespeare, then?' asked Mark.

'I realise you think I'm older than God, but I still have the strength to do you serious harm.'

Mark took a step away from her. 'You should have a word with him, perhaps he'll write a part just for you in his next play.' Mark took another step to make doubly sure he was out of her reach and nodded in the direction of a small group of people where William Shakespeare, in a doublet and breeches of a rich moss green, was chatting to some guests. Bottom was striding around the room with an ass's head under his arm, and Cleopatra, with thick black eyeliner and gold braids weaved into her jet black hair, was entertaining a group of men in suits, although they looked more enamoured with her low-cut dress than whatever she was saying to them. A small group of musicians played a piece of music I recognised as *Greensleeves*, the folksong often mistakenly attributed to Henry VIII. But as was the way at many of these kinds of events, they were largely ignored, their talents serving as no more than background for chatter.

The magnificent Charleton House had been chosen as the host venue for this evening's drinks reception, which marked the commencement of the Derbyshire Shakespeare Festival. For two weeks, theatres, stately homes, gardens, pubs, schools, and even a garage and a telephone box would host performances of Shakespeare's plays. Charleton House had been the home of the Fitzwilliam-Scott family since the late 16th century, and the current heads of the family, the Duke and Duchess of Ravensbury, were known for their love of the arts, so it was the perfect location for the celebration. The reception was also an opportunity to announce that refurbishment was about to commence on the small private theatre that had been added to the house in the 1820s, and that it would hopefully be complete in time to be used as a venue for next year's Festival.

Mark Boxer, my friend and a Charleton House Tour Guide, was taking small groups into the theatre and regaling them with tales of musical performances during the Second World War, of famous theatrical visitors who wanted to see for themselves the magical jewel-like space they had heard so much about, and of Dukes and Duchesses past who had 'trod the boards'. Every thirty minutes, Mark and his latest group would don hard hats and fluorescent vests and head off into what currently amounted to a building site.

I was keeping an eye on some new servers I had just hired, watching as they walked the room offering people canapés of miniature date and quince tarts, little lemon possets and gooseberry fools. As the Head of Catering here at Charleton House, I wasn't just responsible for the three cafés that the visitors used to recharge their batteries with scones and endless cups of tea; I also arranged the catering for smaller events like this, and I had loved every moment of putting together a Shakespeare-inspired menu with my chef. We'd had less fun with drinks, sticking with the usual white wine, but we also had a locally brewed ale on offer, and I watched with some amusement as Shakespeare made regular visits to the drinks table with the silver tankard he was carrying around. It was a good job he didn't have any set lines to remember; I wasn't sure he'd remember his way out of the building at this rate.

'So, where is he, then?' Joyce Brocklehurst, the gift shop manager, was scanning the room. 'Mark tells me you've been getting quite a lot of attention from one of the cast, and I want to make sure I approve before you take things anything further.'

'There's nothing to take further,' I replied. 'He just seems really nice and we chat when he comes in the café, but it's only been about rehearsals, or the weather.'

A promenade production of *Romeo and Juliet*, set in the 1930s, was opening at Charleton House at the end of the week and Capulet – Juliet's father – was played by a rather unassuming man who, along with many of the cast, made regular visits to the Library Café. He wasn't particularly striking looking, but as he was considerate and funny, I'd quickly warmed to him, and we'd bonded over a shared love of good quality coffee, carrot cake and Charles Dickens.

'Richard Culver – he's over there, next to the woman in the bright red shirt.' Joyce stood in silence as she assessed him. It briefly crossed my mind that she would set her own sights on him. Despite being a 'mature' woman of indeterminate age with numerous marriages behind her, she had not given up on finding Mr Right, and was having great fun during her extremely thorough search. With the dress sense of someone half her age, she squeezed herself into eye-catching outfits that showed off her still remarkable figure and made sure she caught the attention of everyone in a room. Her blonde hair was usually tousled, moussed and sprayed into a delicately balanced mass on the top of her head and her nails were lethal works of art, and I loved her. She was terrifying and marvellous at the same time. I was sure that most men felt the same way.

'Hmm, I'm not sure about that moustache...'

'It's just for the play. You don't seem to mind Mark's moustache.'

'Mark's is a superb distraction when he's irritating me. This actor chappie looks like he's balancing something on his top lip. Is the woman he's talking to that Miranda I keep hearing about? She hasn't graced us with her presence in any of the shops.'

The woman next to him had a sharp brown bob and a soft face. She looked at first glance as if she could have been a nursery schoolteacher, if it wasn't for the fact that I hadn't seen her smile once in all the weeks she had been working here.

'Miranda Summerscale, the director, yes. A bit of an ogre, on all accounts.'

'Are ogres women?'

'Well, whatever she is, the Conservation Department are up in arms. She keeps rehearsing in rooms they've told her are off limits and going behind the ropes that are there to protect the furniture. She shouted at a visitor the other day because they walked across the middle of the room while she was "assessing its potential". The visitor must have been all of two years old.'

The theatre company had been given the go-ahead to rehearse during visitor hours, so long as the actors didn't get in the way and understood that our paying visitors took priority between 10am and 6pm. They'd all been briefed on what was off limits and how to help us protect the valuable objects and artwork around the house. I'd heard a lot of comments about how Miranda clearly felt those rules were for someone else. She was also known for screaming at the actors if she wasn't happy, regardless of who was around to witness her temper tantrums. However, despite her personality failings, she was also one of the finest theatre directors in the country and it was a real coup to have her here for the Festival.

My line of sight was suddenly blocked by the Duchess of Ravensbury as she made a beeline towards us in the company of another woman.

'I'll head off,' whispered Joyce. 'I'm not meant to be here; have a good night.' She'd vanished before I was able to say anything.

'Sophie, thank you, the food is as marvellous as ever. I'd like you to meet someone. This is Arianna Mountford, the Director of the Festival. Arianna, this is Sophie Lockwood, Head of Catering. Arianna would like to know if you're willing to share any of your Shakespeare-inspired recipes for an event she's hosting next month, particularly the… Lent pie, was it?

'Tarte Owte of Lent,' I corrected her, quickly explaining that it was made of ingredients you aren't allowed to eat during Lent, such as cheese, cream and eggs.

'Arianna, I'll be back in a moment and we can head into the theatre, but do make sure to get the quince and date tart recipe. I grew the quince myself.'

Arianna was a striking-looking woman. With a mouth too wide for her slim face, she must have been in her sixties and had a wonderful shock of short grey hair. Her long, flowing black outfit was a backdrop to a multicoloured striped pashmina and large plastic earrings that echoed some of the colours in the scarf.

I was back on familiar territory as we discussed the plays I'd used as inspiration for the menu and swapped email addresses as I was happy to assist her in any way I could. Eventually, the Duchess returned and swept Arianna off in the direction of the theatre. It was time for me to check on the kitchen and make sure my team were okay. If there was one thing that could send an event from a raging success to an utter nightmare, it was running out of food and drink.

CHAPTER 2

As the evening wore on, the group thinned out and most of the guests had gone, but a few lingered. Some were deep in conversation while others admired the artwork that lined the walls of the Long Gallery: portraits of Fitzwilliam-Scott ancestors who stared off into the distance, attempting to look noble, but simply succeeding in looking a little vacant, or perhaps irritated that their peace and quiet had been disturbed by the noise of the reception.

Arianna Mountford was talking to the Mayor of Chesterfield who had attended the event in her official capacity, wearing her heavy gold chain of office. They were joined by a bald-headed man who had just walked back into the room. I recognised some of the *Romeo and Juliet* cast who were sitting on one of the windowsills, noticing that one of them had an open bottle of champagne tucked – theoretically – out of sight behind his leg.

Richard ambled over. His linen jacket was heavily creased, but there was something rather charming about it. His smile reached his hazel eyes, and he looked a little bashful, certainly not the kind of actor who enjoyed being the centre of attention once off stage.

'It's been a lovely evening, Sophie. You'll be glad to be rid of us all so you can go home and put your feet up.'

'Not at all – look at the place. Far grander than my sitting room,' I replied. Richard chuckled.

'Grander than any room in my house, too.'

I glanced around the Long Gallery, at the maroon velvet flocked wallpaper and the Grinling Gibbons carvings surrounding the doors, a common feature in many of the rooms at Charleton House.

'Will you at least be able to enjoy a glass of wine now things are quieter? You could join us.' He indicated towards the group at the window.

'Thank you, but I wouldn't be setting a good example to my team.'

'I understand, but when you have finished, perhaps you'd like to join us in the pub. We're all heading to the Black Swan.' He had a calm, soft voice that it was hard to imagine filling an auditorium, but I'd had the chance to watch him in rehearsals where he seemed to change gear and fill the space with a deep, rich sound. I knew he'd grown up in a small town about fifteen minutes' drive from Charleton House, so he was local, but he spoke with the received pronunciation of someone who had been to drama school.

'I'll see what time I leave here, but I'd love to.'

'Great, I'll keep my fingers crossed.' He walked away and the rest of the group stood and slowly made their way towards the door. I gathered up a couple of empty glasses and wondered if Mark would fancy a trip to the pub with me; I was keen to take Richard up on his offer, but didn't feel like turning up alone.

MARK HAD BEEN AWAY for some time with another group at the theatre. I'd helped to tidy up before sending some of my team home; there wasn't much to do now except wait. Eventually, the Duchess made her way over to me.

'Would you mind doing me a favour, Sophie? Mark's current tour is going to be his last; everyone here has seen the theatre, so could you possibly run over and ask him to lock up when he's finished? I'd go myself, but I need to stay here with the remaining few guests.' She lowered her voice. 'I'm beginning to wonder if hitting the fire alarm is the only way I'm going to get them out of here.' She shook her head and gave a little grin. The Duchess is a tall, well-spoken woman with strong, handsome features. She is well used to mixing with royalty and millionaires, but despite the many stuffy situations and formal dinners that are a common part of her life, she is warm, approachable and possesses a delightfully wicked sense of humour.

Charleton House is a vast box of delights of over 300 rooms set within a 40,000 acre estate. About a third of the building is open to the half a million visitors who come every year, but the route to the theatre bypasses many of those areas and runs into the less glamorous places behind the scenes.

Before I disappeared into dusty corridors and up creaking staircases that would need to receive some TLC before the theatre was reopened, I made my way through richly furnished rooms that spoke of the varied and privileged history of the house. I cut through the Music Room with its ornately decorated harpsichords. Further on, I passed through one of the bedchambers, admiring its large four-poster bed with its crimson damask curtains, trimmed with gold lace. Stools and chairs in the room were covered with matching fabric and a card table lined with green velvet stood in a far corner.

I walked past the door to the library and into a long, narrow room that resembled a shrunken, less opulent version of the Long Gallery in which we'd held the evening's reception. It was technically a corridor with the end door only accessible to staff and didn't have velvet on the walls or such ornate wooden carvings around the doors or windows. The dark wood floor matched the panelling on the walls. One side was lined with paintings by Joseph Wright, who had been born in nearby Derby. The subjects of his paintings were often candlelit, and that, along with the dark wood that dominated the room, gave the space a gloomy, shadowy quality.

The visiting public were prevented from getting too close to the paintings by a series of thick red ropes that were slung between thigh-high brass posts. At each end of the ropes, brass hooks enabled staff members to lift them off the posts easily if they needed to inspect a painting or clean the area around it. It was a sombre space that most visitors dismissed quickly, which was a shame as the paintings were deserving of a great deal of time and attention. We referred to it informally as the Wright Room for now; the paintings were to be moved to a more visitor-friendly space next year.

I took in the picture of two girls playing with a kitten and the scene of a blacksmith's shop, running the loosely slung rope through my hand as I went. I could have been walking through one of the paintings, the room was so poorly lit; only enough wall lights turned on to give Mark and his groups adequate illumination to get to the other end, where they would head through the 'private' door.

I was reaching the end of the room when instead of the next rope, my hand felt nothing but air. I looked down. The end of the rope was on the floor. My eye followed its path, and before me lay Miranda Summerscale, crumpled on the floor, the rope wrapped around her neck. There was no visible sign of life.

As I stepped back in shock, the door beyond the body was pushed open and Mark, with his tour group close behind, walked in.

'Sophie!' He beamed as he saw me. 'We're just on our...'

His eyes dropped to the floor ahead of him and took in the sight of Miranda's lifeless form.

'Oh... err...' He spun round to face his group and stretched his arms out, trying to block their view. 'There's something I forgot to show you – please, everyone, back that way... It's really quite marvellous, one of a kind...'

Whatever it was he intended to distract them with might not be as interesting as a dead body, but it would certainly be less horrifying.

CHAPTER 3

I was back in the Long Gallery by the time Detective Constable Joe Greene arrived on site. He came up behind me and put a hand on my shoulder.

'Sophie, what have you been putting in your croissants?' I quickly gave him a dig in the ribs with my elbow.

'Nothing, but I can always change that – just let me know when you're next stopping by.'

He chuckled. 'Sorry, couldn't resist, but this is becoming a bit of a habit. I'm assuming that your security team have sealed off the area?'

'They have. We've also kept everyone who was still at the event or on Mark's tour in here.'

There were about twenty people in the room, including guests and my catering staff. I'd quickly pulled together a couple of tea and coffee urns and laid out the remaining food. Any conversation was quiet and whispered. The musicians had already left and all that remained was a still, fearful atmosphere. Everyone understood that the killer was in all likelihood someone who had attended the reception, but most of the guests had left before the body had been found. We could at least take some comfort from the assumption that the killer wasn't in the room with us, but that didn't stop some from glancing nervously at their fellow guests.

'I wonder if anyone has contacted the cast.' Mark wandered over after pouring himself a mug of coffee. 'I'm not sure how many friends she had amongst them, but this will still come as a shock.'

'Mark, dear,' said the Duchess, who had remained poised and unflustered, 'once the police have taken all the details they need from the remaining guests, would you mind escorting them to the car park? Sophie, I don't think it will be long until your staff can leave.' She rested her hand gently on my arm. 'I know this isn't your first body, but I imagine it's still a shock, so if you need to take some time off…'

She let the suggestion hang. We both knew that was never going to happen. Since I'd arrived at Charleton House, there had been a number of tragic deaths – unrelated to my arrival, I hasten to add, but I had become involved in solving each case. In the silence that followed, I felt that the Duchess and I both acknowledged I was likely to pay more attention to the case than to the job I was paid to do.

'WERE any of the cast still on site?' I asked Joe, handing him a coffee. 'They weren't in here, but they might have been in their green room.'

In theatres, the break room is traditionally referred to as the 'green room', and the *Romeo and Juliet* company had taken over what had once been a billiards room, but now alternated between a storeroom for ladders, a short-term object and painting store, and an activity room for families during school holidays.

'I believe most of them are at the pub, we'll arrange to speak to them later.'

I'm always impressed by Joe's patience with me. He is a good friend and, in all honesty, I rather abuse, or attempt to abuse, our relationship as I try to get information out of him. For a while, we'd come close to being more than friends, but now he's dating Ellie Bryant, one of the Conservation Team, and they seem very happy. After a disastrous engagement when I lived down in London, I'm convinced that I'm more than happy being single, but I do sometimes wonder if maybe I am actively *convincing* myself of that.

My phone rang and Mark's name appeared on the screen. I showed it to Joe, who grinned.

'Tell him not to leave the country. I'll head over to his later and take his statement.' Mark is married to Joe's brother, Bill, so it made sense that he wasn't worried about getting a statement straight away. I guessed he'd combine the statement taking with an opportunity to share a beer with Bill. Hardly police procedure, but a realistic picture.

I answered my phone to Mark's excited voice. 'Hey, Sherlock, I've just taken that last group back to their cars. I thought you might like to know that two of them were talking about an argument they walked in on between Miranda and one of the other guests – they were openly speculating about whether or not there was a connection.'

'Did they say who she was arguing with?' I asked.

'They certainly did. Ariana Mountford, the Festival Director. Apparently, they're known to have a fractious relationship.'

There was a pause as I thought about the woman the Duchess had introduced me to.

'You there, Soph? You're going to get involved, aren't you? One of these days, you're going to take me by surprise and let the police get on with their job; I just can't work out when.'

I glanced at Joe. 'We'll see. The summer season is right around the corner. I've got new staff to keep an eye on and we've got the exhibition in London to start thinking about. It's not the time to leave everything to the café supervisors – I've done far too much of that over the last couple of years.'

'Oh, come on, don't get all professional on me now. This one could be fun. You know I love a bit of Shakespeare; someone somewhere is hoping that a little water clears them of this deed.'

'They're what?' He wasn't talking sense.

'Lady Macbeth, as she tries to scrub the blood from her hands.'

'Miranda was strangled.'

'I know, but I don't know any quotes about strangulation. Come on, you know you want to get involved, and we're bound to dig up some great gossip from within a theatre company.'

'Someone was murdered, Mark; this isn't just about searching out gossip for our own entertainment.' I heard Mark sigh. Fortunately, Joe had stepped away and missed my comment.

'Spoilsport. Look, I know some of the cast are at the pub. How about we head over there and talk to them?' I considered it for a moment, but a wave of tiredness swept over me. This time, even caffeine wouldn't cut it.

'Thanks, but I'm going to head home. Come to the café tomorrow and we'll talk about it then, I'll feel fresher. Oh, and go home yourself. Joe says he'll come round later.'

As I hung up, I looked around the room. Arianna Mountford was sitting quietly with the bald-headed man I'd spotted with her at various points during the evening. The Duchess was deep in conversation with Detective Sergeant Colette Harnby and the Charleton House Head of Security; I guessed the topic of conversation was having to keep a large portion of the house closed to the public tomorrow. Two of my serving staff stood quietly near the tea and coffee urns, looking pale and talking quietly, one chewing her nails and the other turning a teaspoon over and over between her fingers. Charleton House always feels so full of life, whether because of the energy of the staff and visitors, or the stories from the past that we keep alive. Tonight, however, it felt as though a light had gone out, and it had been wrapped in a fog of uncertainty, suspicion and death.

It was time to go home.

IF THERE IS one thing guaranteed to put me in a better mood, it's forcing my cat, Pumpkin, to give me a hug. I found her sitting on the kitchen table, watching a shadow. She glanced in my direction as I walked in, but the shadow was clearly higher on her list of priorities, so I risked Her Majesty's wrath and scooped her up into my arms.

After months of me landing a big kiss between her ears, she'd eventually learnt to present her head to me and allow me to kiss her, before giving a short yowl and wriggling free. Despite her weight, and a belly that leaves me wondering if cat girdles are a thing, she was surprisingly light-footed and flew from my arms, landing directly in front of her food bowl.

'I let you kiss me, now do my bidding and feed me,' was how I read the glare she focused on me.

On the drive home, I had been convinced that all I was capable of doing was falling – fully dressed – onto my bed and descending rapidly into a deep sleep. But after giving Pumpkin some particularly stinky salmon cat food, I opened my laptop and started to scroll through the search results for both Miranda Summerscale and Arianna Mountford. It was easy to find interviews and articles with or about them and gradually pull together a general idea of their careers.

Pumpkin head-butted my leg, hard, and I reached down to scratch behind her ears.

At sixty-two, Arianna was roughly twenty years older than Miranda, but it seemed that her career had lagged behind that of the younger director. Their paths had crossed as they both directed plays for various festivals up and down the country, and they were occasionally nominated for the same awards, but while

Miranda had won a good number of them, Arianna had never taken home a trophy for her mantelpiece. But despite that, and despite not featuring in the glare of the theatre world's limelight, Arianna had a good reputation. Her directing work was considered 'revealing', 'consistent', 'solid'. When it came to the business side, she had turned a number of small, struggling festivals into highly regarded and financially successful events.

Miranda had spent a lot more of her time centre stage, with interviews in Sunday supplements and special features about her on radio arts shows. I wondered just how much Arianna wished her career had followed the same path as Miranda's, whether her work was satisfying or whether she would have liked just a little more of that limelight, and if she had harboured a jealousy that had finally become too much to contain.

I closed my laptop and Pumpkin leapt onto my knee. As she snuggled up hard against me, I wondered whether Miranda's death was the result of a cast member tired of being shouted at, or career-long envy.

CHAPTER 4

I walked across the courtyard in dazzlingly bright May sunshine. The windows of Charleton House all appeared to be mirrors reflecting the blue sky, and the gilding on the frames formed brilliant architectural bling that gave a good clue as to what lay within the walls. This glorious detail was set against the splendid gardens that still maintained many of the features designed by Capability Brown, one of the country's finest landscape architects, when he worked here in the 1760s. There was no doubt that the Duke and Duchess's ancestors had succeeded when it came to creating a status symbol and it was possible to imagine people becoming dizzy with the richness of it all.

Stepping out of the warming sun and into the cold shadows of the cloisters with stone floors out of the reach of the morning heat, I hurried towards the Library Café, my favourite of the three cafés I was responsible for and where my office sat just off the kitchen. I'd overslept and only surfaced when Pumpkin decided she wanted to share my pillow and had almost smothered me with her furry bottom. Not a death I wanted to be remembered by. My hard-working and ever-patient team had the café ready to open as I burst through the doors with five minutes to go, hurling apologies at anyone and anything I passed.

I was handed a mug of coffee by Tina, my long-suffering café supervisor, and a warm croissant by another member of the team. If I'd been awake enough to check, I'm sure I would have seen an amused grin on the face of everyone in the room. I stood in the kitchen catching my breath, the air scented with bacon and sausages ready for our popular breakfast butties.

'Don't worry, Sophie, we're good to go.' Tina had followed me.

'I am *so* sorry, they should fire me and put you in charge.'

Tina laughed. 'No thanks, I've seen the mountains of paperwork on your desk that never seem to go down, and as far as the team is concerned, you are psychiatrist, life coach, guru, keeper of all answers and reason for all problems. Some days, they think you can walk on water; some days, you just can't get it right. I have no desire to step into your shoes, thanks all the same.'

Her response gave me a warm glow. I usually felt like most of the work of a manager went unnoticed; to know there was at least one person who seemed to 'get it' was heartening.

She looked at the coffee mug in my hand. 'Now drink up, and then you'll be safe to appear in front of the customers.' She gave a little smile and left me to it.

As the kitchen door swung to, I heard a familiar voice. Richard was ordering a coffee and croissant to eat in. I made sure my spiky grey hair looked stylishly ruffled, as opposed to dragged-through-a-hedge-backwards ruffled, and attached my name badge to my jacket. I needed to make a vague attempt at leading by example.

'Richard, how are you? Not rehearsing, I assume.'

He smiled when he saw me. 'Fine, fine. No, not until this afternoon. Some of us are meeting with the Festival Director to decide what to do, but we'll all gather this afternoon regardless. Join me?'

I followed him to a table in front of shelves full of countless copies of Shakespeare's plays. The walls of the Library Café are, as you'd expect, covered in bookshelves, and we'd changed the display for the duration of the Festival. It was now almost entirely Shakespeare related. Multiple editions, translations from around the world, cartoon versions, biographies. None of them were financially valuable, but they made for an impressive sight.

'I wanted to come and see how you are; did you not want to take any time off?' Richard held my gaze, concern written across his face.

'No, I'm fine, it all happened very fast.'

'But finding a body, that's shocking. I hope you've been offered some support by the Duke and Duchess.' News, or rather gossip, had travelled fast and I imagined there wasn't a person at the house who didn't know that I was the one to find Miranda's body.

'Thank you, the Duchess did say I could take some time off, but I'm okay. It must have been a shock for everyone in the cast.' It was all I could think to say, even though I imagined there were a lot of mixed feelings.

Richard nodded. 'It's no secret that she wasn't hugely popular, and if they arrested everyone who had declared that they could "bloody kill her", the police would still be investigating the case at Christmas. But she was talented and there was a great deal of respect for her work.'

'Had you worked with her a lot?'

'Yes, and I guess it meant I had more patience with her. I'd watched her career grow first-hand, knew how hard she worked. I tried to protect the others, those not used to her temper. It was never personal, but those who didn't know her well or were still at the start of their careers could take it really hard. I used to tune her out, pretend that I'd just turned her volume off, and she was stood there opening and shutting her mouth like a guppy.' It was heart-warming to hear how he looked out for others.

'Did she ever target anyone in particular? What about during the *Romeo and Juliet* rehearsals?'

Richard shook his head. 'If there's anything positive to say about her temper, it's that she was pretty even with how she threw the insults around. I was just as likely to get it in the neck as anyone.'

'There wasn't anyone in the cast who might have been pushed too far, might have retaliated?'

'You mean killed her?' He sighed. 'I find it hard to imagine. Some of us have history with her, I guess it could have built up over the years. Damien probably has good reason, but I can't imagine any of them turning to murder. Look, I should go. I just wanted to check in on you, but I think I'm expected to take the lead on behalf of the cast, so I can't be late. I hope to see you later.'

As I watched him leave, I made a note to find out more about Damien, and really hoped that Richard had an alibi for the time of the murder.

ONCE THE MORNING rush had died down and the number of staff coming in to hear about my experience of finding Miranda's body had started to dwindle, Joe arrived looking tired and in need of sustenance. He caught my eye, and then took a seat, flicking through the pages in his notebook.

DC Joe Greene had been a regular welcoming face when I first started working at Charleton House. A uniformed motorcycle police officer back then, he'd taken to dropping round for coffee at every available opportunity. But after an intense period of training, he'd been able to transfer and was now a plainclothes detective. I carried over two mugs of coffee and a couple of shortbread biscuits in the shape of Shakespeare's head, and took a seat opposite him.

'Well, she wasn't very popular,' he said without looking up.

'Almost every member of the cast has been on the receiving end of her temper. There have also been a number of paying visitors who have had to be placated with free tickets for another visit after they accidentally walked through a rehearsal and she laid into them. And Ellie – well, I'm surprised she's not a suspect and I'm not having to recuse myself from the case for conflict of interest.'

Ellie's work involved protecting and maintaining the delicate objects, paintings and furniture in the house.

'I take it they had a run in?'

'More than one. The whole cast was provided with training, but Miranda was forever going behind the ropes and getting close to the objects, or going through doors that are off limits, but kept unlocked for health and safety reasons. Ellie admitted to losing her rag on one occasion and shouting at her.

'Miranda was also in the habit of keeping cast members back to work late – clearly no life of her own – and when they worked late, one of the Conservation Team had to work late, too. Ellie had to cancel a number of our dates at the last minute.'

'But Ellie's not really a suspect?'

He grinned. 'No, but I'm going to have a lot of fun teasing her about it.'

'Well make sure you straighten your tie and knock those biscuit crumbs off your jacket, otherwise you'll give her ammunition for a decent comeback.'

He looked down before correcting his tie, looking like a schoolboy who was still getting used to his uniform. At least he'd combed his hair, which wasn't always a given. He never looked messy, just dishevelled, and he was cute too, so he managed to carry it off.

'Is that the only angle you have so far, or have you dug up anything else of interest?'

Joe started to open his mouth, but then paused and looked at me, head tilted.

'Hmm, why do I feel like you're the one digging? Should I be asking you the same thing?'

I feigned shock. 'Never! I'm just innocently curious.'

'That'll be a first.' He laughed. 'All I'll say is that she was local, so we're going to be stretching our questioning beyond the walls of this place, and no, I won't keep you posted.' I pretended to sulk and stole the last bite of his shortbread. At least I knew that I had to look further than a general dislike of her working style as that just led to too many possible suspects.

CHAPTER 5

The kitchen window of the Library Café looks out onto a lane behind the house, and it's here that staff and private visitors enter and exit, so I was able to watch as more of the cast of *Romeo and Juliet* started to arrive just after lunch. I wanted to give them time to gather and start rehearsing, so I finished the sandwich I was eating as I put together an order of coffee. I could manage running out of almost every item we could possibly need, except coffee. That was unthinkable.

I called the Security Office and asked if they knew where the cast had gone. The Long Gallery was the answer and I hotfooted it over there.

The Long Gallery is one space that isn't normally open to visitors, so the cast could get stuck into rehearsing without any distractions, and I quietly entered and made myself comfortable on a low windowsill by the door. Generations of Fitzwilliam-Scott family members loomed out of picture frames. They weren't a particularly good-looking bunch, although the current incumbents were much improved and an attractive family. It seemed the genes had strengthened over the centuries.

As the scene came to an end, Stanley Pickles, who was playing

Friar Laurence, walked over and sat next to me. He was short and tubby with a face like a Brussels sprout. Every time he saw me, his entire face turned into an enormous crinkly smile. Despite being indoors, he was still wearing his tweed flat cap and matching scarf.

Stanley had introduced himself to me the first time he had visited the café and he was a jolly presence when he dropped by. He'd managed to sweet talk me into giving him a mug of hot water each time he came in so that he could drop his own tea bag in it and not have to pay for a mug of tea. I'd never done that for anyone before and wouldn't do it again, but every time I saw him, he made me smile, and he must have bought his own body weight in sausage rolls over the last few weeks, so I turned a blind eye to the lost profits on the tea.

'Sophie, how ya doin? I've been worried. Must have been a heck of a shock, finding Miranda like that.' I nodded and we sat quietly and watched as the next scene started. The nurse was encouraging Juliet to head to Friar Laurence's where Romeo would make her his wife.

'If there's one positive to come out of this, their lives will be a lot easier.' His eyes were fixed on Lady Capulet, who was sitting on the far side of the room.

'Whose lives?'

He nodded in her direction. 'Hannah. She and Damien are a couple, but Miranda hasn't made it easy for them.'

'Why not?' I knew they were a couple, but more than that I was unaware of.

'Damien's her ex-husband. Miranda's, that is. They've been divorced, ooh, two years, but Miranda didn't seem able to let it go.'

'Is Damien in the cast?'

Stanley leant back so I had a clear view down the gallery towards a man sitting on a windowsill at the far end. He was wearing the artist's uniform of thick-rimmed spectacles and a black turtleneck sweater. I recognised him, but had never put a name to the face.

'Damien Fishwick, the designer for this production.'

'But if they didn't get on, why did Miranda hire him as designer? I assume that was her choice?'

'It was. They always kept working together. Personally, it didn't work out, but professionally they were quite the power couple. They don't – I mean didn't – work on every production together, but quite a lot of them, and the results usually included more than one award.' Stanley shook his head. 'Hannah and Damien have been very patient, but it was really starting to get to them. Me too – I like Damien, they make a good couple, and I want my Hannah to be happy.'

I recalled the time Stanley first told me that his daughter was also in the cast. He'd been as proud as punch; he often dropped into conversation how much he was enjoying working with her, and how talented she was. I hadn't seen any physical similarity between father and daughter at first, until I'd seen her smile. She had his eyes, and although I'd only served her at the counter and passed the time of day with her, she was just as warm and friendly.

I took another look at Damien and wondered just how tired he'd become of Miranda's inability to let go. I glanced at Hannah; it was hard to imagine the daughter of someone like Stanley being involved in a murder, but there was no escaping the fact that she might just have a very good motive.

I sat back and rested my head against the window frame as I watched the rest of the scene. It would have been quite enjoyable if the only drama had been of the theatrical kind, but already my cogs were turning, and I was looking at Damien and Hannah in a very different light.

. . .

One of the three cafés I manage sits outside the area that requires a ticket for entry. The Stables Café is located in the imposing cobbled stone courtyard that used to provide a home for eighty horses and the staff involved with their care. I was there making sure my team were focusing on the job at hand and not getting distracted by the gossip that was swirling around about Miranda's death.

'My dad went to school with her.' I turned to face the young man who had spoken. He handed the customer he was serving their takeaway cup of hot chocolate and a bacon butty, and then looked at me. 'Yeah, he said he couldn't remember much about her. She was a couple of years above him, but he's sure it's her.'

'Which school was it?'

'Castledale Secondary.' Miranda really was local – that was only about fifteen minutes' drive from here. Deep in thought, I went in search of a distraction of my own.

Joyce's office was tucked away next to one of the gift shops she ran. Battered cardboard boxes were piled up next to her desk, bubble wrap and tissue paper were scattered everywhere, and she was rifling through a filing cabinet as I arrived.

'Shut the door, will you? I can't think with that bloody racket going on.' I closed the door and the noise of a large group of schoolchildren who were eagerly spending their money on pencils, bookmarks and bars of Charleton House chocolate was muted into the background. 'I'll be with you in a minute, I just need to find someone's file.'

The phone interrupted her search.

'I'm always busy,' she stated firmly to the caller. 'Tell me, Mark, why do you wish to disturb my incredibly precious time?' She smiled at me as she attempted to wind him up. 'Hmm… that's right… agreed, I would. I have to agree – for once – that would be rather nice of you; it will be three of us, though. I have Sophie with me… We are working hard together, you cheeky sod… He hung up on me, the swine. Put your coat back on, Sophie, we're getting a tour.'

Her upper body vanished under the desk and she started rooting around amongst the pile of shoes that she kept at work.

'Where are we going and what are you doing?'

'Mark has a spare half hour and has offered to take us to see the theatre, and I can hardly go in these.' She stuck her foot out to show me the patent purple stilettoes that must have added at least three inches to her height. They weren't the tallest I'd seen her in, but they certainly weren't allowed in the house where there was a risk of her heels damaging the floors.

The Conservation Team had long since accepted that controlling the footwear choice of visitors was an impossible task, but staff were easier to influence. For a long time, Joyce had largely avoided going inside the main rooms of the house on a point of principle. But over the last couple of years, she seemed to have softened to the idea, and now a wide selection of wedge-heeled shoes were part of the jumbled pile of colourful and rather garish ones which had heels capable of taking your eye out if you got on Joyce's wrong side.

With a pair of slightly more conservative, although still vertigo-inducing, shoes firmly on her feet, we set off to meet Mark.

CHAPTER 6

Outside the door to the theatre was a table with a number of industrial hard hats in a variety of colours.

'Grab whichever one you feel best matches your outfit, ladies.'

'I think not,' replied Joyce. 'I'm not wearing one of those things.'

'You can't go in without one,' said Mark, sounding as though he'd expected this response. 'It's not for long.'

I chose an orange one and cringed as I put it on. Who knew what array of sweaty builders had worn this before me? Joyce just stood there, arms folded. Mark stared at her.

'We're not going anywhere until you wear one. If I'm seen taking you in without one, they might stop me doing these tours for staff.'

Joyce said nothing.

'To be honest, Mark, the layer of hairspray she adds to it each day is probably tougher than any of this.' I tapped my knuckles on the top of the hat I was holding out to Joyce. 'You've also emptied enough mousse into it to make sure the weight of the hat doesn't do any damage. I'm sure your beautiful blonde mound will still be visible from space. Plus, it's blue, so it matches your skirt.' It was a tenuous match; her extremely short skirt had been paired with a purple shirt that was covered in gold flecks. You'd be forgiven for thinking she had forgotten to do up most of the buttons, but she wasn't known for leaving much to the imagination.

She snatched the hat out of my hands.

'This *mound* was carefully styled this morning; I don't just empty mousse, or anything else, for that matter, onto it. It's an art form. And my skirt is cornflower blue and this thing is rust-covered shipping container blue.' She was right, it even had the rust-coloured paint splatters on it. 'Alright, I'll concede, a little.' She held the hat about an inch above her head. 'Will this do?'

Mark let out a pained sound. 'Come on, it'll have to.' He led us through a scratched set of dusty brown double doors and I tried to adjust my eyes to the dark. Only one light glowed from the stage, and it didn't help us this far back.

'Ah, hang on, we need more than the ghost light, I'll be back in a minute.' I heard Mark fumble around on the wall, and then with an audible hum and loud clunk, the room was bathed in light.

We were standing under a balcony that ended not too far ahead of us. Rows of theatre seats were hidden under dozens of white dust sheets, and scaffolding stood along the full length of both walls to the left and right.

'Come on, we can't go all the way down, but we can go just beyond the edge of the balcony.'

I looked up, relieved that we weren't going to remain standing under it; I'd hate to test the hard hats.

'What's the ghost light?' I asked nervously. 'Are we not alone in here?'

'Possibly not. There are a few stories about ghosts that spend all their time in here. The light has a couple of purposes, depending on who you ask, but one is that every theatre has a ghost, and the light allows them to perform on stage when no one's around, keeping them happy in the process. Otherwise, they might curse the place. Others say it's simply to scare the ghosts away. In practice, it just means you can navigate the theatre until you find the lights.'

'So, it's not haunted?' I was a bit disappointed.

'I never said that,' Mark replied with a wicked look on his face. 'The ghost of one old fella is meant to make the occasional appearance. Back in the 1870s, the nephew of the 8th Duke was appearing as Hamlet. He used a real skull for the famous *Alas, poor Yorick* scene – it wasn't unusual for real skulls to be used and no one knew who the skull belonged to or where it had come from.

'Anyway, the nephew had recently had a falling out with one of his cousins. It turned out the cousin had broken into the family mausoleum, got his hands on the skull of one of their relatives and swapped it with the skull they'd been using for rehearsals. He was found out when the mausoleum was discovered to have been disturbed and the errant cousin's pocket watch was found on the floor. He quite proudly admitted what he had done, claimed it made the performance of Hamlet even more of a family affair. Rumour has it that the ghost of the body in the mausoleum is often seen in here, trying to find his head.'

'Didn't they put it back in the mausoleum with the rest of his skeleton?' I could have done without hearing this story, but couldn't help being fascinated.

'They thought they had. But when the cousin was an old man, he admitted he had put the original unidentified skull in there. It seems he was determined to keep his practical joke going. Who knows how many additional stage appearances the unfortunate relative has made over the years?'

Joyce looked horrified. 'Do you have any stories that aren't quite so morbid?'

'A couple, but I don't get the pleasure of watching you go pale if I tell those.'

'That's simply the light in here, your ridiculous stories don't disturb me one jot,' she insisted.

I looked around and tried to see beyond the scaffolding and decades of dust. It resembled a Victorian toy theatre.

'The archway is lovely,' I said, wishing I could get a closer look at the ornately carved and beautifully painted gold plasterwork. The rich red of the tasselled curtains didn't seem to have been too ravaged with time. 'Have the curtains been replaced recently?'

That prompted a broad grin from Mark. 'Clever, isn't it? They're not real. I can't get you any closer, but the whole thing – the proscenium arch and the curtains – is a *trompe l'oeil* painting. It's an illusion – it looks 3D, but get up close and it's flat.' It was quite simply stunning. The ceiling was decorated with painted panels that depicted Derbyshire landscapes, but some of the paint was starting to peel and I knew it would take quite a bit of work to get it back to its original glory.

'It was built in 1837 for the 7th Duke. The one who drove his mother nuts because he never married. He was a bit of a polymath: fascinated by science, spoke numerous languages and loved the arts. There was a rumour that he was in a relationship with a famous actress and spent time with her when he was in London, but I've never found solid evidence.

'His nieces and nephews would put on plays here, and many of the following Dukes and Duchesses have trod the boards, as children and adults. Both Edward VII and George V were treated to performances when they visited. Dame Ellen Terry made a visit, Sir Henry Irving accepted an invitation. It was in regular use until the 1970s. In fact, I think the current Duke was one of the last people to perform here, when he was about nine years old. I've seen photos of him. Quite the little star he was, too.'

'Yes, I'm hoping to get him up there in the future.' I jumped; we hadn't heard the Duchess come in. 'I don't think it will take much, the Duke enjoys an audience. Sorry, we didn't mean to interrupt.' *We* included two men in suits and Arianna Mountford. I spotted Joyce let go of her hat and allow it to rest, gingerly, on her hair, which did appear to have crumpled a little. She looked very uncomfortable.

'It will be marvellous to see it in use again. We have so many plans. Sophie, do you ever perform? You gave such a wonderful reading at the Christmas service, I could imagine you'd be perfect for staff shows here.'

Just the thought made me feel queasy, but I didn't want to dampen the Duchess's enthusiasm, so I just smiled sheepishly.

The Duchess and her group stepped away and walked to the other side of the seats, where they rolled out some architectural plans across a board that was resting on the seat backs.

'Will we see you up there?' I asked Joyce. She could hardly be called a shrinking violet at the best of times and she had performing in her blood: her mother had been a dancer and had performed as part of the Tiller Girls in London's West End and on tour. She peered at me out of the corner of her eye.

'Unlikely. I like to maintain some dignity in my advancing years, and I wouldn't want to put everyone in the shade.'

'I'd grab the moment, if I were you,' suggested Mark. 'You don't know how many of those advancing years you've got left.'

'More than you'll ever have, Mark Boxer.'

I left the pair of them bickering and tried to get as close as possible to the Duchess and her guests. The two men in suits were now pointing at the front of the balcony and were too far away to hear, but the Duchess and Arianna had pulled back one of the dust sheets and were sitting in two end seats facing the stage. Arianna was talking about her plans.

'...I think it's important that we open with *A Midsummer Night's Dream* – it was the first play ever staged in here, so that would be perfect symmetry. I already have a couple of casting ideas, but we'll have to move quickly as it's only twelve months away.'

'I would like the local community to be involved,' added the Duchess.

'Of course, Your Grace, I thought we could use local people for the mechanicals.'

'*Duchess,* please! You can call me Your Grace at more formal events, but as we'll be working together a great deal now, let's keep it less formal.'

'Of course, Your Gra... I mean Duchess.'

The Duchess turned to face Arianna, and I moved closer to the wall to avoid being in her sightline.

'Look, I want to be frank with you, and reassure you in case it was on your mind. You are well aware that we were also discussing this role with Miranda and had yet to make a decision when she died. You are, naturally, the obvious choice now, but I don't want you to think you have been offered the opportunity to relaunch this theatre simply because the other candidate has been so sadly and horrifically killed.'

Arianna bowed her head slightly. 'Thank you for that, I do appreciate it. I also want to make sure that, in some way, we remember Miranda. I was thinking perhaps a Shakespeare Festival prize in her name would be appropriate.'

I quietly stepped away and went to join Mark and Joyce as they walked out of the door, Joyce pulling the hat from her head as soon as she crossed the threshold. So, Miranda and Arianna were both being considered as the director of the opening production in the theatre once the renovation was complete. Getting that role would pull Arianna back into the limelight and help put her on a par with Miranda, had she lived. As I removed my hat and tried to fluff up my now squashed hair, I wondered just how badly Arianna had wanted the role.

CHAPTER 7

I looked at the line of beer pumps. You could order a pint of 'Macbeth'; there was also the simply named 'Shakesbeer' and 'Romeo's Poison'. The local breweries had gone to a lot of trouble to get into the Festival spirit. Sadly, no gin distillers had done the same, so I wasn't drinking a bard-inspired gin and tonic. Mind you, the Black Swan pub had a list of over seventy gins, so I was hardly limited in choice.

After our tour of the theatre, Joyce had swiftly returned to her office, only to find that her emergency can of hairspray would do no more than splutter and cough, so she spent the rest of the day hiding from colleagues and customers alike with hair resembling an unrisen cake. As soon as she could, she'd scarpered home.

Mark and I, on the other hand, opted to head to the pub. With my usual plate of fish and chips in front of me, and Mark tucking into a large slice of steak and ale pie, I told him what I'd overheard before leaving the theatre.

'Will it really make that much of a difference to her career?' Mark asked as gravy dripped down his chin.

'Possibly. She was always a step or two behind Miranda, and then a couple of years ago, she seemed to stop trying to compete, if that's what she was doing. At any rate, she moved up here to Derbyshire and worked in a couple of theatres in Manchester, Leeds and Sheffield until she got the job running the Shakespeare Festival. She was gaining a very good reputation up here, but the reality still seems to be that it's viewed as "regional theatre" and you have to fight to be considered in the same class as anything in London. It's that blasted north-south divide again, this country can be so London-centric.'

Mark eyed me over a forkful of chips.

'Can I get you a soapbox to stand on?'

'It's true, same with restaurants. We're chipping away at it, but it's slow going. Anyway, think about it. Charleton House is considered one of the finest historic houses in England. You told me these private theatres were quite rare here, more common in houses of mainland Europe, so this one is also unique. There have been some pretty impressive actors treading its boards and we know that there is already a lot of press interest and a plan for at least one documentary to follow its final few months of completion and reopening. There's also bound to be a pretty senior royal coming to see its progress, one in particular who is known for his interest in architecture and restoration of historic buildings.

'It would be quite a coup for her to get the job over Miranda, who is local to the area. Even if it wasn't a huge boon in terms of her career, Arianna would be able to make quite a personal stab at Miranda, and that would no doubt sting, a lot. So, it could simply be bitterness on the part of Arianna, no more than that. But we know that people have killed over much less.'

I stuffed an enormous piece of fish in my mouth. It didn't matter how many times I ordered the fish and chips, I never got bored with it. The beer batter was crispy, and I knew the landlord made sure the fish was as fresh as you could get without living next to the sea. Sadly, I was increasingly having to undo the top button on my trousers when I ate it. Not that that would stop me.

'What about that lot?' Mark nodded in the direction of the group of cast members who had just walked in. Juliet, or rather the actor playing her, had gone to the bar while the rest settled round a large table. Clearly not thirteen years of age like her character, she carried a large tray of drinks and a couple of bags of crisps to her colleagues. 'You don't think that a moment of anger after being verbally beaten down throughout rehearsals was enough to make someone wrap a rope around her neck?'

'I do, and I still don't know what their alibis are like.' I was mainly wondering about Richard's.

'Finish eating that whale-sized portion and let's go and find out.'

'Are you calling me or the fish whale-sized? And remember, I'm holding two sharp implements.' Mark paused a little too long, so I playfully stabbed him in the back of the hand with my fork.

'WILL THE SHOW GO ON?' Mark asked the assembled cast members who had welcomed us to their table enthusiastically. Richard had looked particularly pleased and had quickly moved up to make room for me next to him.

'It will,' replied 'Juliet'. 'It didn't seem right to do anything else. We're close enough to opening night that we can get by without a director, and we know it's what Miranda would have wanted. There was no debate.'

'It must help that you have each other's support through this.'

Stanley, still wearing his flat cap and scarf, nodded. 'You become quite close very quickly during rehearsals, and in her own way, Miranda brought us all together. Shared experience of her tempestuous personality.' He gave a wry smile as he looked at his colleagues.

'What about the fear that it might have been one of the

company?' It was a risky question, but I was desperate to know if any of them had their suspicions. None of them flinched.

'We all have alibis, of one kind or another,' explained 'Juliet'. 'Most of us were in the courtyard – we were going to the pub, and some of us had waited outside for the others. That accounted for everyone here, except Richard and Stanley. But we could see Richard in the window of the room we were using as our green room. He was there for the whole period that the police say she would have been killed during.'

Richard turned to me. 'Miranda felt I was increasingly "lacking energy". I was in there going over some lines, trying to figure out what she meant. I was just stood by the window with no idea what was going on.'

I felt a weight lift from my shoulders.

'And I was already at the pub.' Stanley raised his pint in the air as 'Juliet' continued.

'Damien and Hannah left after the rest of the group. They were together so have each other as alibis, but even so, Damien was often the most supportive of Miranda. Along with Richard, he was always talking people down off the ceiling and trying to get them to the point where they could understand her a little better. He'd never want to hurt her.'

Stanley turned to me. 'Didn't I see you talking to that detective constable in your café? The young one who doesn't seem to know how to iron a shirt.'

I laughed at the description. 'Joe – I mean DC Greene, yes. He's a friend of mine.' Out of the corner of my eye, I noticed Richard quickly look at me. I wondered if he was jealous.

Stanley dug a bit deeper. 'Did he give anything away? Do they have any ideas?' His question reminded me that I should give Joe a call; I wanted to know what the police were thinking, and I hadn't spoken to him for what felt like ages. It was time to see what I could get out of him, although I wouldn't be passing any information on to the cast. Joe was risking enough trouble as it was when he spoke to me; I didn't want to put him at any more risk of reprimand from his superiors by then spreading around whatever he told me.

'No, and he wouldn't tell me even if they did. I have no idea what's happening.' Half of my response was true.

Eventually the conversation turned to other subjects: theatre, beer, where those less familiar with the area should go for hikes, what it was like to work for the Duke and Duchess. Richard was gracious and funny and made sure I felt included in the conversation. It was, to all intents and purposes, a lovely evening with lovely people, but the subject of murder hovered permanently at the back of my mind. I couldn't help but wonder if this close-knit group of friends and colleagues would be prepared to help one of their number cover up a crime. They were actors, after all; they had the perfect skills to help one of them avoid arrest.

CHAPTER 8

I lay nose to nose with Pumpkin and had done since she'd woken me half an hour ago by leaping onto the bed and sprawling on top of me, her face shoved up close to mine and a paw around each side of my neck. She wasn't always quite so sweet, so after some slow, careful manoeuvring which resulted in me being able to reach the alarm clock and turn it off without annoying her, I revelled in her own version of affection. She's heavy enough to affect my ability to breathe, but as she hasn't actually suffocated me – yet – I decided she could stay.

As I lay there enjoying the sound of Pumpkin's purring, I recalled that Shakespeare didn't seem to be keen on cats and tended to talk about them negatively in his plays. They were used as insults in *Romeo and Juliet,* so as much as I liked his work, I'd be hard pressed to like the man.

My thoughts turned from *Romeo and Juliet* to the cast of characters that had appeared in Charleton's own theatrical tragedy, and their motives, but so far it was just a jumble of quarrels, bad tempers and career-based jealousy. All of which could easily result in murder, but none of which struck me as particularly noteworthy in this real-life production.

I scratched the top of Pumpkin's head with some force. She wasn't a delicate cat and didn't need delicate handling. Part of the problem was that I didn't have a very clear picture of Miranda; I needed to find out more about her, and if there was one person who would know her *very* well, it was her ex-husband, Damien.

Wednesday morning started with a flurry of meetings. The roof above the Stables Café had leaked during an overnight rain shower and a wine rep wanted me to taste some new white wines he felt would be perfect for our more upmarket Garden Café. The Duchess was eager to replace the outdoor furniture at the Stables Café despite the fact the season had already begun, and it would have been helpful for her to have determined this over the winter months so we could have started afresh with it at Easter.

When I finally returned to the Library Café at 11.30, I was pleasantly surprised to find Damien Fishwick had taken over a small table and covered it with sketches and plans.

'Can I refill your coffee cup?' I asked him, still clutching the notebooks and papers I'd walked in with.

'Thank you, I'd appreciate that.'

After dumping my coat and paperwork in my office, I returned with two mugs of coffee. I was getting low on caffeine and wanted to wash away the taste of wine. I might have only been slurping and spitting, but 10am had been too early for alcohol; I did have some limits, despite what Mark and Joyce might say.

'Can I join you?'

Damien looked surprised, but removed his bag from the chair opposite so I could sit down.

'Last minute changes?' I asked, looking at the drawing laid out between us.

'Just some small adjustments to the lighting.' He looked tired. The thick rims of his spectacles couldn't hide the deep shadows beneath his eyes, he was pale, and against his black turtleneck sweater, he looked gaunt.

'It must be hard to concentrate.'

He nodded. 'It has been. But the show must go on.' He smiled weakly.

'What was she like? I've heard quite a lot, but it's all pretty much the same. There must have been another side to her.' I was trying to be diplomatic.

'What you mean to say is she can't have been so horrible all the time. I know what people say, I've said it myself many a time. And as you also probably know, I was married to her, so I know exactly what she was like. But you're right, she wasn't like that all the time.' He took a long drink of coffee, and then settled back in his chair. 'She was really excited to be back here. She grew up just down the road in Castledale, so there were countless family visits to the house when she was young. She often talked about staging plays here, so she was ecstatic when her schedule finally worked alongside that of the Shakespeare Festival. She directed her first play in Castledale, so it's rather fitting that she was directing what turned out to be her last here.'

'Was that at school, the first play?'

'It was. The English department organised regular coach trips to see the Royal Shakespeare Company in Stratford-upon-Avon, so she saw her first Shakespeare at fourteen. *As You Like it.* From that point on, she was obsessed. She told me her bedroom walls were covered with posters for the RSC, not pop bands. She read everything she could get her hands on about Shakespeare, and as soon as she could drive, she used to take herself off on overnight trips to Stratford, stay at a local B&B and see a Friday night performance, followed by a Saturday matinee and a Saturday evening performance. Sometimes they'd all be of the same production if she was particularly enamoured with it.

'Luckily, the school had a very good theatre of its own and she started directing her own productions. Not just Shakespeare, also some Oscar Wilde, a Harold Pinter, Caryl Churchill. She wanted to stage a Sarah Kane, but one of the parents got wind of it and soon put a stop to that. Funnily enough, she was about to stage a Shakespeare – *A Midsummer Night's Dream* – when the theatre burnt down. The school caretaker died and the building was completely destroyed.'

'My God, that's awful. Did they find out what happened?'

'It was assumed it was bored local kids, although they never caught them. There had been a fire at a church hall in the next village over, which the police said had been started in the same way. It stopped after the school fire – maybe they'd freaked themselves out once someone had died.

'They were lucky more weren't killed – Miranda was there with two of the cast. They'd finished rehearsing and most of the group had gone home; the caretaker had allowed the three of them to stay a bit longer while he tidied up and got ready to lock up for the night. The place was in semi darkness and the police thought the kids probably believed the building was empty because the cast were quiet, making notes or reading, so they didn't know anyone was in there. Thank God Miranda and her friends got out.'

He drained his coffee cup and I sat in stunned silence. As he'd talked, some of the colour had returned to his face; perhaps he had needed a distraction of sorts.

'She told me she cried as the theatre burned. Some of the schoolchildren who lived nearby had turned up and were loving the fact that part of the school was burning – nothing malicious, but hey! The school's going up in smoke! I'm sure plenty of children hope for that on a daily basis. But Miranda had fallen in love with the theatre. It didn't matter that it was a small school theatre.'

Damien started to collect his papers together and put them in a file. He brightened as he continued.

'They rebuilt the theatre, made it state of the art, and Miranda put on *A Midsummer Night's Dream* as its opening production. She was due to go back next week – they're renaming the theatre after her and she was to give a speech before a play put on by the students as part of the Shakespeare Festival. She was really moved by it; she was desperately keen for young people to get involved in theatre and be introduced to Shakespeare in a way that dispelled the idea of it being dry and unintelligible. It's even more poignant now, the naming.'

He pushed his chair back. 'Thank you.'

'What for?'

'Giving me a chance to talk about the other Miranda. The one who people tend to forget, who is less fun for people to gossip about. She was challenging, I won't deny that, but the theatre has lost someone with a real passion for its future.'

I watched him leave, so glad I'd spoken to him. There had been a risk that I would have just taken all the gossip as read, and then assumed that the killer was simply an angry cast member who could no longer take being shouted at. But Miranda was as complex as anyone else and there was a lot more to her.

But what about Damien? He clearly admired his ex-wife, but was it enough to take him off the list of suspects? I cursed myself for not thinking to ask about Miranda's attitude to his relationship with Hannah, but he had seemed happy to talk to me and might open up about other subjects now we'd shared this moment. I'd catch up with him again as soon as I could; I felt as though there was a lot more I needed to learn from Damien.

CHAPTER 9

Mark had finished eating his salmon and fig pie, although a fair amount of the pastry was now scattered across his shirt, and there was no doubt plenty in his lap as well.

'Not bad. A little unusual with the cinnamon and ginger, but the combination of flavours actually works really well. Shakespearean?'

'Tudor. I tried to get as many ideas as possible from his plays, but I saw this and knew it was worth a try. They're based on *nese bekys*, but they were usually deep fried, whereas I baked these.'

'Well, it was a dish fit for the gods,' he declared dramatically.

'Shakespeare?' He'd taken to quoting his plays at every available opportunity. It was just on the edge of getting annoying.

'Correct, *Julius Caesar*. I'd eat another, or are you afraid,' he paused, 'I will eat you out of house and home?'

'Go on,' I said wearily.

'*Henry IV part II*. I could go on all day.'

'I'd be grateful if you didn't.'

'But isn't it fascinating? It's believed he introduced more than

1,700 new words into the English language. He created countless phrases that we continue to use.'

'And in some cases, overuse.'

'I'm getting into the spirit of things. We should take this opportunity to reacquaint ourselves with his genius, fully engage in an excess of bardolatry.'

I sighed. 'Oh, for goodness' sake.'

'Ha, that was one of his, *Henry VIII*. But going back to that pastry, it was good. I could eat another.' If that was a hint, he was out of luck; I gave him enough freebies as it was, so I ignored his comment.

He wiped his hands on a napkin and started to flick through the pages of the programme for *Romeo and Juliet*.

'For once, a programme that isn't just full of adverts. Mind you, it is ten quid. You could buy a book for that.' I could see page after page of glossy photographs. 'Hmm, nice picture of Richard.' He spun it around so I could see a black and white photograph of a moustache-free Richard looking moody. 'It would have been more appropriate if he was playing Romeo, but he's far too old.'

'Take that smirk off your face,' I told him.

He turned the page and spent a moment looking at a full-page picture of Shakespeare. It was the commonly used Chandos portrait and I'd seen the original in the National Portrait Gallery when I lived in London.

'Do you think he's where they get *egghead* from?' I asked.

'Hmm, perhaps, he is rather cranial.'

I enjoyed my coffee while he scanned the pages, his attention landing on a number of lists in small print.

'It always interesting to see who has paid for things. These are sponsors both for *Romeo and Juliet* and for the theatre renovation. There are a few new sponsors, but a lot of these are familiar names: a couple of solicitors, an architect's firm. Excellent – the Bakewell Brewing Company are one of the big sponsors, which means we're bound to be serving their ale in the interval. Now then…' He ran his finger down the lists, and then back up to the top of the page. 'Here we are, this is what I was looking for. This is interesting.' He spun the programme around again so I could take a look and placed his finger next to a name. 'Look familiar?'

'Mountford Enterprises,' I read aloud. 'Mountford, as in Arianna?'

Mark nodded. 'Her brother, Maxwell.'

'I wonder if that was the bald man I saw her with at the reception on Saturday night.'

'Probably,' Mark agreed. 'What category is he in?'

I checked. Donors were grouped depending on how much money they had given, and each group was named after a part of the house or gardens.

'The Gilded Hall,' I told him.

'Which means?'

'I guess it means he gave quite a lot of money as it's close to the top.'

He turned the programme back to face him. 'Correct. He must have given over twenty-five thousand pounds to end up in that category, which is unusual. It's not uncommon for him to donate money – I'm told he doesn't have the slightest interest in art and history, but does it simply to keep his name in the "right circles". Only, I don't recall him ever giving more than ten thousand, and it's usually more like five. Don't you think it's curious that he dug considerably deeper into his pockets for an event that has some connection to his sister's work, and when his sister is under consideration by the Duchess for the role of director of the opening production at the theatre?'

'He might just be supportive of Arianna's work. It doesn't seem that strange.'

'True, but it might be more than that, and he might be doing everything he can to get her in the Duchess's good books.'

He was right, it was interesting.

'Okay, I'll concede, it's worth looking at. We need to try and find out more about him.'

'Sophie,' Tina called out to me as she walked towards us.

'Ah, something wicked this way comes,' Mark said in a low witchy voice.

'I beg your pardon?' She was more than used to Mark.

'*Macbeth*, act four, scene one.'

'Ignore him,' I told her with a shake of my head.

'I usually do. Look, I couldn't help but overhear your conversation. You do know my sister is working in the office.'

'Which office?' I asked.

'The Shakespeare Festival office. She took on a temporary admin job for the run of the Festival and she's practically Ariana's PA. I'm sure she'd be keen to try and help you out.'

A sudden jolt of excitement ran through me. I wondered if this was how dogs felt when they got a scent.

'I wouldn't want to get her in any trouble.'

'Are you kidding? I've told Ruby all about you, she's often said she'd love to find herself involved in sniffing out a killer.' It was hardly surprising that I was getting a bit of a reputation as the local Sherlock, but it wasn't something I wanted to be known for. It wasn't like I sought out opportunities to solve a murder.

Tina took a pen out of the pocket on her apron and wrote a phone number down on a napkin. 'I don't know how much she can help, but she'll just be pleased to meet you.'

'My dear Tina,' Mark said with a dramatic lilt to his voice, 'you have a heart of gold, and with your help, the game is afoot. In one fell swoop, Sophie will now be able to prove that this is not a wild goose chase.'

'Go on.' I offered, reluctantly.

'*Henry V*, *Henry IV*, *Macbeth* and our very own *Romeo and Juliet*.' He looked very pleased with himself, but Tina was stony-faced when she replied.

'Mark, if only you understood that brevity is the soul of wit.

Hamlet, act 2, scene 2.' She turned and calmly walked away to the sound of my applause.

'Hey, whose side are you on?'

'Stop showing off. Are you coming with me?'

'Not if you're going today, I have a couple more tours booked in this afternoon.' He turned and looked me in the eye. 'I shall head forth into a brave new world…'

'Shut up.' I threw a screwed-up napkin at him and heard him mutter *The Tempest* as he walked away.

I briefly felt guilty about once again leaving Tina to run the café in my absence, but as she'd suggested I call Ruby, she clearly wouldn't mind. I would see if Ruby was free tomorrow; I was keen to know more about the Mountford family and just how ambitious the siblings were. I was also concerned about what this meant in relation to the Duchess. Even if Arianna was second choice and only got the job as a result of Miranda's death, the idea that someone had attempted to sway the Duchess's decision-making with a financial incentive, and then got the outcome they wanted anyway simply muddied the waters. I was going to have to be really careful if I wanted to investigate that any further.

CHAPTER 10

The nurse was complaining about her aching back while Juliet badgered her for news of Romeo. Small groups of visitors to the house had gathered in a courtyard to watch the rehearsal. A couple of teenagers had settled down on the ground, leaning against a stone wall, and appeared to be as enthralled as they would be by any Hollywood film.

I waved at some colleagues who had opened a window and were watching the scene unfold. I was meant to be delivering coffee to Joyce, but I forgot all about that as I was pulled into the drama.

The cast weren't in full costume, but just enough to affect the way they moved. The nurse was wearing a long apron over her modern clothing and Juliet wore a long skirt over a pair of leggings. A couple of the male actors were watching from the side in Homburg hats. Stanley was also watching; he had put on a friar's habit, but I could see the bottoms of his jeans and he wore a tatty pair of trainers.

He spotted me and walked over.

'Hello, Sophie,' he whispered. 'What d'ya think? It's coming along nicely, isn't it, and it's so good to have these little impromptu audiences. It really helps us inject a bit more energy into it all.'

'It's been fun watching bits like this, but I want to see it all together now.'

'You could stay behind one evening, watch a dress rehearsal. I don't think anyone would mind.'

'Thanks, Stanley, but I'd like to save it for Saturday.'

'I understand. I'm sure you'll enjoy it. Damien has worked wonders with the lighting, and the soundscape really lifts it.' His face crinkled as he smiled; he looked genuinely excited and proud of what the group had achieved.

'Stanley, do you have a couple of minutes? I'd like to ask you something.'

'Of course.' He stepped away from the audience and I followed him to a bench in the corner of the courtyard. 'How I can help?'

'How did Miranda seem to you in the run-up to her death? I'm just wondering if there was something or someone bothering her.'

Stanley looked down at his hands and appeared to be examining his stubby fingers before sighing.

'You know, it still feels very unreal. I keep expecting her to come round a corner and scream that we're doing something wrong. I never thought I'd say this, but I miss that. I actually want to be shouted at now.'

He looked up at me. 'Why are you so interested?' There was only curiosity in his voice. I'd never been able to adequately answer this question when asked in the past; something just kept pulling me in, getting me involved.

'Curiosity, wondering why I ended up with a dead woman at my feet. I want to know the whole of the story.'

He nodded; he could probably relate to the story aspect.

'Miranda largely kept her private life to herself. Of course, I knew more about it than most because of Hannah and Damien, but it would have been unlike her to let on that there was a problem, so I could only assume that everything was fine.'

'What about outside of work?'

'Oh, we didn't see her outside of rehearsals, not much. She came to the pub a couple of times early on, and then left us to it, but that's typical for her.'

'How was she the last time she went out with you all?'

Stanley gave his chin a thorough rub; it looked as though he hadn't shaved for a day or two, and I heard the rough bristles against his fingers.

'That was a good few weeks ago, but if I remember rightly, she was in good spirits. Well, by Miranda's standards. She bought a round of drinks and left some money behind the bar when she went so we could get another one in after she'd gone. I don't recall her saying much to Damien or Hannah, but she was alright with the rest of us. She was talking about getting a tattoo, so those of us who have them were pulling up our sleeves or the legs of our trousers to show off what we had. One of the younger lads pulled off his t-shirt to reveal quite an impressive tiger on his back.'

'Doesn't that affect your ability to get work? If the tattoo isn't right for the character?'

'Makeup, my dear, it's amazing what you can do these days. Most of them were small things; the tiger was a bit much in my view. Your Richard has a nice one on his arm.'

'*My* Richard? We're not…'

'I'm teasing, dear. I remember her asking him if tattoos could cover up scars.'

'Why would she ask that? Did she have one, a scar?'

He nodded. 'She had quite a bad fall as a teenager and ended up with a metal pin in her arm; the surgery left a noticeable scar. I didn't think it bothered her, but maybe it did.'

'Did she talk about anything else that sticks in your mind? Did she ever seem worried or distracted?'

'Ha, she was permanently distracted – by the words, the poetry, forever examining and critiquing. It was like she existed on a different plane when we were in rehearsal. I'll be honest with you, Sophie, if there really was something bothering her, we'd have been hard pressed to tell. She was so intense, so involved in her work that she could be quite a difficult person to read. Until she screamed at you, of course.' He laughed. 'Then you knew exactly where you stood.'

He put his hand on my knee. 'I need to get on, I'm in the next scene. Come find me if I can help with anything else.'

Miranda seemed a little more human each time I learnt something new. She might have been obsessed by Shakespeare as a teenager and appeared supremely confident, but she still had accidents and insecurities about her appearance. The more I developed a clear picture of her human side, the more I felt sorry for her and wanted to find out who had killed her.

CHAPTER 11

'Whoa, what's the rush?'

I pulled back, apologising profusely to whoever I'd nearly run into with two take-out cups of hot coffee. I'd drunk Joyce's coffee as I watched the rehearsal, so I'd returned to the café, got caught with serving a long queue, and it wasn't until two hours later that I was able to make my way towards her office, only this time I'd had the sense to make a coffee for myself, too.

'Sorry, I was miles... oh, Joe, it's you.'

'Yes, it's me, and no need to sound less apologetic as a result. I'll assume one of those is for me.'

'It was for Joyce, but...'

He took the cup from my hand before I could argue. Oh well, Joyce would have to go without, again. She didn't even know she was getting it, so no harm done.

'Walk with me back to the car, it's a lovely day.'

We dodged chattering school groups, made way for elderly ladies with walking sticks and nodded our hellos to colleagues on their way to meetings. Charleton House was definitely a community all of its own, whether members of that community lived here, worked here or were just visiting for the day and would never come again. A blue sky always gave the place an extra dose of energy – staff walked a little quicker and laughed a little louder. It even seemed like the ideas came more readily in meetings and it was easier to negotiate and find a happy medium on which to agree.

The honey-coloured stones of the main building glowed, the flowers in the window boxes explored the air around them, and windows that had been closed for months were given a firm shove and finally opened. It made it easy to forget that only two nights ago, someone had been found strangled and their murderer was still free to walk the streets, and maybe even continue to walk the corridors of Charleton House.

We strolled in companionable silence for a little while, Joe presumably going over details from the case. But I couldn't muster the patience to wait for long.

'How's it going, anything interesting?' I asked, trying to sound vaguely disinterested. One corner of his mouth turned up as he sipped his coffee.

'Not bad, roughly two minutes before you broke.'

'I'm impressed with myself.' I laughed.

'Slowly is how it's going. It turns out the theatre world is quite small. Most of the people at that reception had links to Miranda, a few were from London and had crossed paths with her there. She was local so had connections with people and places round here, too. Added to which, the guest list wasn't being checked thoroughly. We're not aware of anyone entering who shouldn't have, but we can't rule it out. There were just so many people who could have left the reception for five or ten minutes, had an argument with her, killed her, and then returned to enjoy another glass of wine. The way she died means they would have had to have been quite strong. It would take a bit of effort to strangle someone with a rope that thick.'

'So the killer is a man then?'

'Not necessarily, but they'd need to have a reasonable amount of strength and my first assumption would be that the killer was male. They also wouldn't have any blood on them. They might have built up a bit of a sweat as they strangled her, but that's easier to hide than bloodstains, and the tour groups were taken that way earlier, so what we might normally consider evidence could have been trailed through by almost anyone or disturbed by anyone in the group.'

We'd left the main gates to the house and were walking up the hill towards the car park. We stepped aside for a coach full of tourists, and I watched as one of our security team had strong words with a journalist who must have been sniffing around. Instead of a juicy headline, all he got was a finger wagged in his face and, knowing the security officer concerned, a rather colourfully worded order not to return again.

'Are you narrowing it down at all?'

'We are.' He sounded confident. 'We're also keeping that information firmly within the police, not sharing it with the local amateur Sherlock.' He tilted his cup towards me. 'You may be a very good amateur Sherlock with an irritatingly good clear-up rate, but you're still closer to possessing a deerstalker than a warrant card.'

'I'll focus on the compliment rather than your lack of generosity. Who on earth would want to come on site for an event like this if they weren't invited anyway? It's not like there were any celebrities there – well, not of the conventional kind – so getting past a poorly managed guest list wouldn't seem worth the trouble. You'd also need to know your way round in order to find her away from the main reception, so you'd have to be familiar to Charleton House staff and at least some of the reception guests.'

Joe was staring at me. 'Do you ever switch off? We are paid to do this; you don't need to bother.'

'You'd like that, increase your chances of figuring out who did it.' I playfully leant into him. We'd reached his car and he handed me his empty cup.

'Tell Joyce thanks for the coffee.'

DESPITE IT BEING MID-WEEK, the car park was busy and I cut across a patch of grass to avoid the cars ignoring the 5mph signs. Up ahead, I spotted the long blonde hair of Hannah Pickles. I sped up and fell into step behind her.

'Hannah, hi.' She looked momentarily confused, and then recognition spread across her face.

'Sophie, right?'

'That's right. It must be good to know the play will still go on. But only two more full days of rehearsals. Are you nervous?'

'Always.' She laughed. 'I figure that's what keeps me going. Nervous energy.'

'I'm guessing you'll have good audiences, with all the extra coverage.'

'Yes. We were close to selling out anyway, but I think any available tickets have gone to those more interested in Miranda's death. Sad, but true.' We were close to the main entrance and Hannah was pulling her temporary staff pass out of her bag ready to show it to the front-of-house staff checking tickets. Mine was already hanging around my neck.

'To think you almost witnessed a murder, you were leaving right around that time.'

She looked a little shocked at my comment. 'Yes, I suppose. Oh, you found her, that must have been awful.'

'You and Damien left together, I believe?'

'Yes, a group of us had been collecting our coats and bags. The others left to go to the pub, but Damien and I were going straight home, so we took our time.'

We were about to step through the doors into the house when

an older woman with white hair managed to get Hannah's attention.

'Sorry, just a moment.' The two women chatted briefly, gave each other a hug and Hannah returned with a bag. 'Part of a costume,' she explained.

'Who was that?' I asked, looking back at the large woman in a shapeless smock dress and pale pink cardigan.

'Ginger. Miranda's landlady while she was staying here. The Festival office provides a list of places actors and crew can stay. A lot of them are locals who rent spare rooms out during events like this. Miranda really lucked out. She doesn't drive and Ginger agreed to drive her to and from work if she couldn't get a ride with one of us. She – Ginger – also helped out with some of the costume alterations. Nothing major, but she was a seamstress and has been able to solve a few problems for us.'

'Did she ever come to rehearsals with Miranda?'

'Yes, she helped Miranda carry things in from time to time if she had a lot of stuff with her, and she'd stay and watch for a while before going home.'

'Do you have a number for her? I'm dreadful with a needle and thread. Having someone who might be able to alter a few clothes for me would be incredible.'

'She's mainly retired now, doesn't take much work in, but she's very kind. I imagine she'll be happy to help.'

I fancied a bit of a drive in this sunshine, and there was every chance Ginger would know about some aspects of Miranda's life that didn't make it to the rehearsal room. As soon as I'd got her number, it would be time to put one of my own personal 'Watsons' to work. Joyce would hate Ginger's taste in clothes, but I guessed they were somewhere in the same age range and Ginger might open up to Joyce a bit more than to me. It was worth a try at any rate.

CHAPTER 12

It had taken two minutes for Ginger Salt to see through my charade of phoning to ask if she could do some alterations to some of my clothes. I'd made the most of the opportunity to ask a couple of questions about her link to the production of *Romeo and Juliet* – too many, it seemed – and she had quickly declared that she knew I had no interest in her skills with a needle and thread. She was as sharp and direct as Joyce, only she sounded much less terrifying.

By the time I asked Joyce to come with me to meet Ginger for tea at hers, I wasn't quite so sure if it was such a good idea. Chances were I was going to spend the next couple of hours watching a verbal sparring match and not get a lot more out of it than sheer entertainment. But Joyce was more than up for it, stating that I was unlikely to get anywhere without her help. It was, however, on the condition that she could drive.

The spring sunshine had lit up the rolling Derbyshire hills like a flawless film set. The jumbled crisscross of silver-grey dry stone walls divided fields into an uneven patchwork of green, and the grassy banks at the side of the road held bursts of mellow colours. I thought I saw some purple and white flowers, but blasting along the 30 mph zones of the country lanes at 50 mph, with the roof of Joyce's BMW convertible down and my hair behaving like a spin cycle on my washing machine, made it hard to see clearly. Joyce had had the sense to secure her locks with an animal print headscarf, carefully chosen to match her animal print bolero jacket and animal print shoes. I clung on to the door handle for the fifteen-minute journey and prayed that every police officer in the area was distracted by the hunt for Miranda's killer.

Joyce brought the car to a stop outside a small stone cottage and I straightened up my glasses and attempted to pat my hair down. A neat white picket fence framed a garden that held beds of hardy geraniums, pinks and peonies. A number of large terracotta pots were filled with different kinds of lavender and one corner was thick with a variety of grasses. When I'd returned to Derbyshire I'd known almost nothing about gardening, but over the last two years, the Charleton House head gardener had been trying to educate me. My own garden was still dreadfully neglected, however.

In the middle of this sweet cottage garden was a rough circle of gravel, and dead in the centre of that, a small white wrought-iron table with three matching chairs, swirls and loops giving the heavy furniture an elegant touch. Ginger opened the door as we pulled up, wearing the same shapeless dress and pink cardigan as she'd had on earlier. She took a moment to scrutinise the car, and then Joyce, who removed her headscarf with a dramatic flourish.

'I thought for a moment it was the Duchess herself who had come to see me.' I caught a look of pride on Joyce's face, only to see it dashed as Ginger continued, 'Only she's a bit more subtle. Come on, girls, I thought we could sit out here, shame to waste the good weather. Take a seat, I'll be right out with drinks. Tea? Coffee?'

We crunched over the gravel and sat down.

'I think we should call the police,' whispered Joyce. 'The style police. It looks like she woke up, crawled out of bed, and then just tossed one of the sheets over her. That's not a dress, it's a shroud.'

'Sshhh. Not everyone was born with your innate sense of... well, ability to find colour matches that no one else ever knew existed. It's a remarkable talent, Joyce, and not everyone has it.'

'I don't think that was as complimentary as it sounded, but I'll overlook it this time. Either way, that woman needs my help.'

'Here we are.' Ginger reappeared with a tray of mugs and a cafetière. Up close, her hair was a mixture of white and silver. It didn't quite reach her shoulders and hung in messy, thick waves. 'I pulled out the chocolate Bourbons, because everyone loves a Bourbon.' As she placed the tray on the table, I noticed her hands. They looked strong, browned by the sun, the nails short and neat, a few scratches on her fingers. These were hands that took on the gardening, built walls, put up shelves and tried to fix things when they broke down.

Ginger looked at the leopard print stilettoes encasing Joyce's feet. 'Would you like me to get them a bowl of water? Saucer of milk?' I tried very hard not to laugh, but my shaking shoulders gave me away and I received a very stern glare from Joyce.

'Only kidding, love, I think they're marvellous. I have some leopard print cushions inside. I like to make a statement from time to time, I just don't like to scream it across the rooftops. Now, Sophie love, instead of messing about, why don't you just get straight to the point and tell me what you want to know?'

I liked Ginger immediately; she was direct, but not cruel, and when she focused her slate blue eyes on me, I knew she was truly listening.

'I believe Miranda was lodging with you for the duration of the Festival, but she grew up here, so did you know her before?'

'I've known her most of her life. Her aunt used to live next door, so I watched her grow up. I hadn't seen her for... oh, now, twenty-five years? Once she upped sticks and went to university, that was pretty much it. I only saw her in passing after that, and then never again. Seems she recognised my name on the list of lodgings and gave me a call.'

'What about family, are they not around?'

'No, her aunt moved to Nottingham, but I believe she passed a few years back. Her folks went down to the south coast; I think her dad's passed, too. As far as I know, her mum's still alive.'

'Did you know her well enough for her to confide in you if she was worried about anything?'

'Do you mean did she tell me someone was out to kill her and she might not make it to opening night alive? Sadly not, nor did she tell me who hated her enough to kill her. We were close, but not that close.' Somehow, Ginger managed to make sarcasm sound kind. 'We did spend quite a lot of time together. I'd give her a ride to Charleton House if no one could pick her up, I'd pour her a glass of wine when she got in, and I helped out with some of the costumes. We weren't bosom buddies, but I knew her of old and she was always a good kid. A bit intense, especially once she got involved in the theatre, and even as a young 'un, she didn't suffer fools, but I was never on the receiving end of her temper.'

In my mind, I ran through the list of people who might have had a reason to want Miranda out of the way.

'Did she talk about Damien, her…'

'…husband. Now, that she did. One night, we shared a bottle of wine… well, two. It might have been three, now I think about it, and she talked about him then. She was never one to get emotional, not the soppy kind, but it was clear she missed him. It seems they had one of those intense love-hate relationships. Couldn't live with each other, couldn't live without.

'Eventually, Damien made the break, but they kept working together. They would never get back together, though, despite all the time they spent working side by side. Miranda used to tell me that it wouldn't work, even if they had the chance to try again, but that didn't stop her wondering about that possibility. Of course, he'd met that Hannah girl and it sounded serious. By bottle number three, she admitted that she'd done a few things to try and throw a spanner in the works.'

'What kind of things?' Joyce had leant forward in her chair; she liked a bit of second-hand drama.

'She'd keep Hannah working late so she couldn't make dates with Damien. Miranda had done the same thing when she was working with Damien back in London, trying to make sure he was busy when Hannah wasn't working.' Joyce looked disappointed; it clearly wasn't gossip as juicy as she'd hoped. 'It wasn't nasty, vicious stuff, but after a while, I'm sure it got very tiresome. Miranda had come to regret all of that, and she told me how rotten she was feeling. She knew it was time to move on.'

Ginger topped up our mugs with what remained of the coffee, glancing over at Joyce at the same time.

'What dress size are you? No, don't answer that, I think I can tell. Could I borrow you for a while?' Joyce looked confused. 'I need to alter a dress before tomorrow and you're a similar size. I could do with having someone put it on to make sure I've got it right. It's based on a 1937 Vionnet dress Wallis Simpson wore, and I'm trying to get the hem right. I reckon you'll look a darned sight better in it than Lady Montague will; you've got great posture, she has a very slight stoop. It'll be nice to work on someone who really knows how to wear clothes.'

That had her; the slightest compliment about her wardrobe or figure and Joyce was putty in the speaker's hands.

'I'm sure I can manage that.'

'This evenin' alright? Only I need to get it back up to the house tomorrow for the dress rehearsal.'

Joyce looked over at me. 'I'll need to drop Sophie off, and then I can come back later.'

'Fabulous, only you might want to change your shoes, otherwise you'll scare the cat.' Ginger cackled at her own joke. I expected to see Joyce's face fall, but instead she threw her head back and joined in.

'Don't worry, it's not the shoes it needs to be afraid of, it's the dragon who's wearing them.'

'Now, now.' Ginger waved her finger up and down the length of Joyce. 'I can tell, as much as you rather enjoy pretending to be the dragon lady, there's a pussycat under that leopard print.' Ginger was treading on thin ice; Joyce definitely liked to keep any squishy parts – literal or metaphorical – well hidden, so I was shocked when she replied.

'You've got the measure of me, girl, but tell anyone and you'll be closely acquainted with the dragon lady.'

Ginger pretended to shudder. 'You're scaring me now.' They both laughed; I simply sat and stared at them. It normally took Joyce weeks, months or even years to soften towards someone. As much as I knew she loved Mark, she still to this day played the hardened harridan around him, and she didn't exactly give me an easy time. But this was different. She appeared to be taking Ginger in with genuine curiosity, and smiled at everything she said. She hadn't even made an unsubtle dig about Ginger's outfit to her face. I was tempted to ask if she had been taken over by aliens, but I didn't have time as she stood up.

'Come on, Sophie, sooner we go, quicker I can get back. How about I stop off on the way and pick up a bottle of wine?'

Ginger gave her a thumbs up. 'Make it white and I'll let you in the house. Red and you can drink it on your own out here.' It wasn't in the slightest bit funny, but they both guffawed. I was starting to feel like a very confused gooseberry, but I did as I was told, thanked Ginger and got back into the car. I was developing a much clearer picture of Miranda and the different sides of her personality. Joyce, on the other hand, was leaving me thoroughly baffled.

CHAPTER 13

'I don't know what was going on, it was weird.'

I was sitting across from Mark in the Black Swan pub. He was nursing a pint of Romeo's Poison and I had my usual gin and tonic. Each time I came in, the landlord would choose a new one for me to try, but I wasn't keen on this one: Stanage Dry Gin. Named after a gritstone edge popular with walkers in Derbyshire, it was far too heavy on the minerals for my liking and each mouthful tasted as if I'd just licked a piece of slate.

A couple of locals were propping up the bar of our cosy pub, the smell of wholesome home-cooked food bursting out from the kitchen every time the door opened. Recently polished horse brasses that had been attached to some of the wooden beams reflected the warm yellow light, and although the fire hadn't been lit, the large open fireplace provided a central focus to the room. It was the ideal place for me to end the day, and living over the road meant I didn't have far to stagger if I had one too many.

'Do you think she fancied her?' Mark asked with a heavy look of confusion. I nearly snorted the gin out of my nose.

'Joyce the man-eater? Are you kidding? Even if she did swing both ways, I can't imagine she'd be interested in someone with Ginger's dress sense, unless she saw her as a project.'

Mark looked into his pint glass. 'I've only had one of these, and yet I'm thoroughly confused.'

'Don't worry, it's not the beer.'

He took an enormous gulp and left a line of beer froth across his moustache. Picking up a napkin, he dabbed it carefully.

'Moving away from the slightly disturbing topic of Joyce's sexuality, did you learn anything useful?'

'Yes and no. Nothing that helps me point a finger at the killer, but I do get the sense that Miranda was a lot nicer than people realised – she wasn't an evil child who pulled the legs off insects. She was passionate about the theatre, hugely dedicated to her work and extremely ambitious. I'm starting to rule Damien and Hannah out, as much as they had the opportunity and motive. All that was messy and I'm sure upsetting at times, but so are many relationships and their breakups. Damien clearly didn't hate Miranda, or I didn't get the feeling he did.

'I think the murder was work related. She'd been crazy about the theatre since she was a teenager, she never hid her ambition or passion, she was a huge success, but sadly at the expense of other people's feelings. I'm sure there are plenty of people who were just plain jealous. That's where I think we should be looking, and I know who we should be looking at.'

Mark raised his eyebrows at me over his glass. 'Are you going to tell me or do I need to add a truth serum into your gin?'

'If it would make this taste better, then please do.'

'Hello, Sophie, Mark.' I hadn't noticed Richard enter the pub.

'Richard, join us.' Mark made room for a third chair and gave me a sly smile.

'Thank you. I can only stay a minute, it's Hannah's birthday and they're about to bring out a cake.'

I looked across at the group of familiar faces who were

getting comfortable around one of the larger tables. A tray of drinks was being carried over by Damien.

'We were just discussing professional jealousy.'

'Now that's a subject that could keep us going all night,' Richard replied as he smiled at me.

'I get the impression Miranda was successful from the very beginning?' I asked him. 'When she was directing plays at school.'

Richard nodded. 'It was a lot of hard work, though. Even at school, she was a taskmaster, but we all wanted to be involved.'

That stopped me. 'You knew her back then? Wait, I know you grew up round here... was it in Castledale? Did you go to school with her?'

'Yes, didn't I tell you?' That explained why he knew her so well, why he was so patient with her temper and able to do such a good job at supporting those unused to her outbursts. He'd known her throughout her career. 'It's really thanks to her that I do this now. She cast me in her school plays and I got the bug. Instead of going to university, I went to drama school. I owe Miranda a great deal.'

I could see a flicker of light behind the bar as someone lit the candles on a cake.

'I should go. Forgive the noise that's about to follow, there's no way this lot can sing quietly.' He gave my arm a very light squeeze as he got up.

Mark waited until Richard had reached the others, and then fluttered his eyelashes at me.

'Romeo, oh Romeo.'

I hit him. 'I don't know why I didn't think of the school connection earlier.'

'Because you can't see past his hazel eyes. You're distracted by your desire to reach out and touch his... moustache while he reads Shakespeare's sonnets to you by candlelight. Before the pages go up in flames and instead of the aroma of his musky aftershave, you end up with the smell of charred facial hair stuck in your nostrils for the rest of the night.'

'I don't know how Bill puts up with you. Or are you speaking from experience and you've had to be doused with a fire extinguisher before now?'

'Close. I did wake up to one of my teenage nephews trying to set fire to the end of my 'tache with a cigarette lighter when I fell asleep after dinner one Christmas Day.'

'I hope he got a good telling off.'

'No, Bill walked in the room with the blow torch he'd used on the crème brûlées and offered him that.'

'Did they manage to…?'

'No, but I've never fallen asleep at a family get-together again.'

Our conversation was interrupted by a loud and beautifully sung rendition of *Happy Birthday*. Hardly surprising as almost everyone in the group must have had singing lessons at some point during their training. The cast looked happy and relaxed, which was good to see; it had been a stressful, upsetting few days for them.

Once the singing stopped, Hannah blew out the candles and kissed Damien.

'Who is it you think we should be looking at?'

'What?'

'Before we were so rudely interrupted by your suitor, you were about to tell me who you thought deserved a bit more of our attention. Who is it?'

'Who was Miranda in competition with for a high-profile regionally and historically significant job?' He looked blankly at me across the table. 'I really think we should focus our attention on Arianna and Maxwell Mountford. The Duchess had talked to both Ariana and Miranda about who would direct the first production when the Charleton House theatre reopens next year. With Miranda out of the way, the job landed in Arianna's lap.'

CHAPTER 14

I fancied a change of scenery, so I had arranged to meet Mark and Joyce for morning coffee in the Garden Café. In a previous life, it had been an orangery. Built in the 1700s as a conservatory for delicate plants, it had been heated with stoves in winter months. It must have been an eye opener for those unused to the sight of such exotic plants – it would have housed orange and lemon trees, cacti, succulents, palms, yuccas, orchids... the list went on and on. The plants were a testimony to the courage of the collectors, the gardeners' skill, and the wealth and status of the patrons. It was only right that they were housed in an equally splendid building.

Now it served as the most upmarket of our cafés. The white tablecloths, sparkling glassware and polished cutlery were the backdrop for afternoon teas with delicate pastel-coloured petits fours and little sandwiches with their crusts removed. Champagne was savoured in celebration of events large and small, ladies who lunched shared gossip and couples stared into one another's eyes as their steak bavette or seared scallops went cold. Here my staff wore crisp white shirts and I always had a quick look to see if their shoes were polished and their nails neatly trimmed.

By eleven o'clock, half the tables were filled, and out on the patio, between the orange and lemon trees, a few hardy souls braved the slightly chilly morning temperatures. The day's cooler weather had been reflected in Joyce's choice of outfit: an *extremely* low-cut cream mohair top paired with a long cream skirt. She'd added a wide red belt which had the overall effect of making her look like a slice of Victoria sponge cake. The bright red leather bag hooked over her arm looked expensive and I wondered if my month's rent would cover the cost. Once I spotted the logo, I concluded that it was unlikely.

'I wanted to show you something I found…' Mark was scrolling through some photos on his phone as Joyce thanked the server who'd poured her coffee.

'Have fun last night?' I asked Joyce, as keen as Mark to know how her evening had gone, but being a little more delicate about enquiring than he would.

'You know, I haven't laughed that hard in a long time. Two bottles of prosecco helped, of course; I was very pleased to discover that she enjoys a bottle of something sparkling as much as I do. She's a dab hand at cocktails, too, so we finished the evening with a couple of Brandy Alexanders… don't look at me like that! I had a feeling the fizz might flow, so I abandoned the car and got a taxi over to Ginger's. It was marvellous, we're already planning a few girls' weekends away. We were thinking London first, some shows in the West End, The Ritz for afternoon tea, the American Bar at the Savoy for cocktails.'

'Then why are you so damned perky?' The jealousy rang loud and clear through Mark's question. 'I'd be face first in that Danish pastry, snoring before the coffee hit the bottom of my cup if I'd drunk as much as you two last night.'

Joyce fixed him with a firm stare. 'One, years of practice,

stories of which would make your eyes water. Two, I have the constitution of an ox, never been sick a day in my life. You, on the other hand, have the constitution of a dormouse and are so wiry you're not fit to serve as a draught excluder.'

'Oh, really? I'll show you, Black Swan tonight…'

'Children, please.' I laid a hand on Mark's shoulder. 'There will be plenty of opportunities for you to get blind drunk and make a fool of yourself in the years to come. Joyce, about Ginger…'

'I admit, I need to work on her style, but once she got talking, I swear I didn't even notice that dress.'

'Did she say any more about Miranda, anything that might be useful?'

'We didn't talk about that. We do need a night off from all this murder business. It was wonderful to find someone truly on a similar level to myself. Don't get me wrong, Sophie, you're marvellous company; it's just that Ginger and I have so many shared experiences, and we are a little closer in age. I'm much younger than her, of course.'

I gave Mark a kick under the table, a warning not to make any age-related jokes. 'You really did hit it off!' I was genuinely pleased for her, if a little surprised. I had never heard her speak about any female friends, mainly just a long line of men as she dated one after the other and tossed them aside.

'She reminds me of my sister in so many ways.'

'I didn't realise you had a sister. Perhaps you should introduce them.'

'I'd have a job, Bunny died over twenty years ago.'

Mark looked up from the cinnamon swirl that he was slowly pulling apart with his fingers.

'Oh, I'm sorry. Were you close?' As I asked, I realised I knew almost nothing about Joyce's family. A little about her mother, but beyond that, she was a blank page.

'Very. She was only a year younger than me. Very different, on the surface much quieter, and like Ginger, she wasn't particularly interested in fashion, but she had a wicked sense of humour that would make your hair curl, and as a child was the first to lead us into all sorts of scrapes. It was cancer that got her in the end. When she died, I swore that I would live life enough for the two of us. That's why you'll never hear me say that I'm bored. If I find myself at a loose end, I ask what Bunny would have done, then I go and do it.'

I wondered if that was also why she dressed the way she did, as though life was exploding out of her wardrobe. Joyce took a sip of coffee before turning to Mark, who was gazing intently at her.

'Mark, dear, you were going to show us something.' She patted his arm, seemingly telling him she was alright.

'Was I? Oh yes, it doesn't matter, really.'

We spent the rest of the hour gossiping about two members of staff in the finance department who we were convinced were having an affair, and talking about a production of *Macbeth* that was being performed in the grounds of a ruined castle. We had tickets for next week and were hoping the dry weather would hold out for the early evening production, although we'd be sure to take plenty of layers and a hip flask of something warming.

Eventually, Joyce left for a meeting, and I watched heads turn as she walked between the tables towards the door. Joyce wasn't a large woman, but she had plenty of curves, and her choice of outfit tended to show off each and every one. It was both impressive and extremely distracting.

As soon as she was out of sight, Mark whipped out his phone.

'This is what I was going to show you both before Joyce made it clear that Ginger is her new bosom buddy. You've not said anything about this, so I guess that Ginger didn't tell you yesterday.'

As I read through the article, my heart sank. If there was more to it than met the eye, I didn't want to be the one to tell Joyce.

The article described the night of the fire at Castledale School, ending by talking about the caretaker who had died. How dedicated he had been, how loved by the students and teachers alike. He was described as forty-three years of age, single and with no children. He had, however, left behind a sister. His name was Leo Salt, his sister was Ginger.

I removed my glasses and rubbed my eyes, trying to think what this might mean and why Ginger hadn't said anything about him. It might be as simple as her finding it too upsetting to talk about.

'I wonder if this was something else they bonded over, the loss of a sibling?' Mark suggested.

'But why didn't Joyce mention it?'

'She seems pretty caught up with this newfound friendship, perhaps she doesn't want to even consider Ginger's involvement.'

'Do you think she might be?'

'Well, it seems like a bit of a coincidence that Ginger's brother died in a school fire that was started the night Miranda was there rehearsing a play, then almost thirty years later, Miranda is killed while staying in her home.'

He was right.

'We need to talk to Ginger again, but I think we should tell Joyce first. She'll be upset with us if we don't and it might be that she can get Ginger to open up, especially if it's a subject she's reticent to discuss.'

Mark sighed. 'I'm not looking forward to this.'

I knew exactly how he felt.

I TOOK the long walk back to my office, stopping off at the security gate to catch up with Roger, my favourite of all our security officers. I considered him one of my chief 'testers' and often dropped by with cake or cookies. His wife was a keen baker, too, and his waistline showed the effects of two women spoiling him with baked goods.

He showed me some photos of his six-month-old grandson and told me how adorable he was. Whilst we were talking, I watched Ginger pull up in her car. She waved enthusiastically at me before handing a dress in a protective bag over to a member of the *Romeo and Juliet* production team. Presumably it was the dress that Joyce had helped her alter last night.

I chose not to take the opportunity to talk to her about her brother; it would need some delicate handling and I didn't want to ambush her.

Roger waved at her as she drove off.

'Do you know Ginger?' I asked.

'A little. I've seen her around over the years, but more since she's been helping with the play. I had to tell her about that director gettin' killed.'

'How come? I'd have thought one of the cast would have phoned her.'

'Well, she was 'ere. She'd come to pick up Miranda. Like her personal taxi service, she was. She was waiting, and of course Miranda didn't appear when the event was meant to finish at nine. Ginger came to ask me if the reception was over or if they'd decided to rehearse late. By that time, you'd already found her and we'd called the police.'

'How long had she been on site?'

'Let me think. I'd just come back from doing me rounds and I walked across the front of the building. She was parked up by the entrance to the car park – I remember cos I waved. A little while later, you radioed us about the body, and shortly after that, she came to talk to me. Now, you radioed at nine minutes past nine; I remember that cos I wrote it down and realised it was one of those palindrome things. So working backwards, I must have walked past her car at about eight-fifteen. Is it important?'

I paused before shaking my head. 'No, it just helps me work

out the order of a few things.' Roger didn't look convinced, but I didn't want to put any ideas in his head. He's a lovely man, but the security office is a hotbed of gossip. The last thing I wanted was a rumour flying around that Ginger was the killer, but sadly, that was the thought now lodging itself in my head.

CHAPTER 15

I watched as the actor held the champagne bottle carefully in his left hand and rested a heavy-looking sword against its side. He took a deep breath before running the sword along the bottle at great speed. The cork, and glass rim, shot into the air and his actions were met with whoops and cheers.

'Careful, careful,' a voice shouted as someone picked up the cork, still stuck within the glass rim that had become detached from the bottle. 'Don't cut yourself.' The champagne was poured into a number of waiting glasses.

'Waste not, want not,' called the actor who had so spectacularly opened the bottle.

'What's going on?' I wasn't surprised by Mark's appearance at my side; I'd watched him enter the gardens in the far distance with a small tour group whom he had now released to enjoy the scents and sunshine as the day started to warm up. We were on the far side of a low wall in an area of the maintenance yard where the public were not permitted. The Charleton House Health and Safety Manager was standing off to one side, watching to ensure that every cork that flew into the air, and the glass attached to it, was immediately retrieved.

'He sabres a bottle of champagne in the opening scene and he's practising.'

'He does what?'

'Sabres the bottle.'

'Never heard of it.'

I turned to face him. Mark is a sponge for both fascinating historical facts and utterly useless titbits that he attempts to impress people with. I couldn't recall the last time that I knew something he didn't. It felt particularly satisfying.

'Sabring – well, it's actually called the art of *sabrage*. Sliding a sabre – although they're not using an actual sabre – along the body of the bottle to break the collar or "annulus" away. It's ceremonial, started under Napoléon. Look, he's going to do it again. He holds the bottle in his left hand, with his thumb up the punt…'

'The what?' Mark looked at me, bug eyed. 'The punt? And he's doing this in public?'

'It's the dip in the base of the bottle. Now, shut up and watch.'

For a second time, the cork and glass collar shot into the air.

'Surely you end up with bits of glass in the bottle and you've just wasted a good champagne?'

I shook my head. 'The force of the pressure pushes it all away with the cork. It's perfectly safe to drink.'

He turned to face me. 'You're very knowledgeable about all this. Do you possess a skill I have, until this point, been blissfully unaware of? Am I going to have to start inviting you to all my parties to impress the guests?'

'Of course I know about it, I've worked with food *and* wine most of my adult life. Yes, I've sabred a few bottles in my time, and – more importantly – I seriously hope you haven't been hosting parties and neglecting to add me to the invite list.' I peered at him through half-closed eyes.

'Chance would be a fine thing. Bill would kill me if I didn't invite you.'

We stood in silence, watching a number of the actors taking it in turns to have a go at wielding the sword. A line of open bottles of inexpensive sparkling wine was growing.

'I wonder if they're going to drink all that?' Mark mused. He pulled a pocket watch on a chain out of his waistcoat. 'Hmm, 1pm. It's a bit early.'

'It's 5pm somewhere in the world,' I confirmed.

We were interrupted by another whoop as Richard shot the annulus off his bottle with the skill and flourish of an experienced sabreur. After accepting the congratulations of his colleagues, he turned towards me and, catching me watching, smiled. He handed the sword to Stanley who pretended to fight with a lawnmower before taking hold of a bottle.

'You know, we've been missing the blindingly obvious,' Mark said, sounding suddenly serious and keeping his eyes on Stanley. 'If Damien and Hannah were keen to get Miranda out of the way, then it stands to reason that her father might be of the same opinion. They seem very close, and if he can help his little girl achieve happiness – or in this case, marriage to Damien, which I assume she considers to be one and the same thing – then surely he'd go to the end of the earth to do so.'

'I thought about that, but he went straight to the pub ahead of the others, where he must have had at least a dozen witnesses, and was waiting for Damien and Hannah when they arrived.'

Mark smiled. 'What if they were in on it? Steve is a busy landlord, he's not going to notice what time everyone comes and goes, and whether or not Hannah and Damien are in on it, or agree with what he might have done, surely they would want to protect Daddy? He could easily have left the group, claiming to go ahead. He secretes himself somewhere out of sight and waits for an opportunity. He then leaves unseen by the rest of the cast and hotfoots it to the pub. So long as he gets there before everyone else, he's covered.'

'Not if there are customers who clocked exactly what time he arrived,' I suggested. Mark shrugged.

'So he stopped to admire the view.'

'In the dark?'

'There were sheep on the road, the car broke down temporarily, he got lost, he sat in the pub car park taking a phone call. There are dozens of scenarios he could describe to the police that would excuse any timing discrepancies.'

Mark brought his list to a close as Richard walked over to join us. He reminded me a little of Joe before he'd become a detective and lost some weight. The amount of time Joe had spent on a motorbike, combined with regular visits to the café, meant that he'd previously had the look of a teddy bear about him. Definitely not overweight, but a little soft around the edges, and Richard had a similar physique. In fact, there was quite a lot about him that reminded me of Joe.

'Mark, Sophie, not bad, eh? Although I have to confess, I've done it before – nearly took someone's eye out that time.' He pulled a face of mock horror and I laughed.

'I'm glad we're out of doors, then, and all the way over here.'

'Definitely for the best. Do you want to have a go? I'm sure no one would mind.'

Before I had a chance to reply, Mark spoke up. 'Sophie's a bit of an expert at it, I'm sure she'd put you all in the shade.'

'Really? Then I don't think I should risk the embarrassment. I thought I was quite good, but I have no doubt you'd wipe the floor with me.' He paused. 'I got some good news today: I've been cast in a production of *Hobson's Choice* at the Leeds Playhouse, so I'm going to be in the area a little longer.'

'That's fantastic, congratulations,' I replied, immediately realising I sounded as pleased as I felt and that Mark was going to make me pay for it.

'Well, I should get back. See you later.' He hesitated again, as though he wanted to say something else, then smiled and jogged back to where the others were gathering up errant corks and another member of the cast was being given instructions.

'Really?' Mark eyed me suspiciously. 'Really? He's a grown man, wasn't that a little pathetic?'

'What?'

'He was nervous – he wanted to ask you out. Mind you, it sounds like he's going to have lots of time to practise his opening line now he's staying around.'

'What can I say? I make men nervous.' I put a hand on my hip and pretended to lean seductively against the wall.

'Are you okay? You look like you've got indigestion.' I swatted Mark's arm. 'I completely understand your effect on men. You make me nervous, too, whenever you offer me one of your latest attempts at a new baking recipe.'

'That's done it. I was going to invite you back to the kitchens this week for that exact reason. But not anymore.'

'What are you making?'

'Chocolate mashed potato cake.'

Mark rolled his eyes at me. 'I rest my case.'

CHAPTER 16

The Derbyshire Shakespeare Festival offices were situated in the spa town of Buxton, on the first floor of an elegant straw-coloured Georgian house. On the upper floors, rows of large sash windows basked in the sunlight. A line of beautifully preserved rounded arches on the ground floor formed the entrance to a covered walkway at the front of the building. Baskets of red geraniums hung from the ceiling of the colonnade.

Immediately opposite stood the exquisite Buxton Opera House, an Edwardian masterpiece designed by Frank Matcham, one of the most important theatre architects of the time. When the doors opened in 1903, it was considered a splendid gem amongst the mill towns of the area. But it was the perfect match for the other listed buildings in the town that made its mark as a tourist destination for the wealthy visitors of the 18th and 19th centuries who wanted to experience the famous thermal waters in Buxton's spas.

The theatre's domed towers frame its grand entrance with its ornate glass canopy, and its Edwardian patrons would have stepped through the doors into a foyer of white marble, Turkish carpets and silk brocades, the walls covered with leather paper. The auditorium's domed ceiling is decorated with painted panels that represent literature, dancing, fine art and poetry. Outside and off to one side are the Pavilion Gardens, beautiful parkland always packed with picnickers in the warmer months. These days, children love the miniature railway and families share leisurely rides on the boating lake.

I stood under one of the archways below the Festival office, leaning against the wall and people-watching as I waited for Ruby to come down. I'd called her after finding a parking spot and she'd told me to wait outside; we could go for a coffee in the tearoom under the offices.

I'd never met Ruby before, but I knew who she was as soon as I saw her step out of the door. She had the same slight build as her sister, and the same neat, short brown hair. Her smile was a mirror image of Tina's. We shook hands and she led me into the café where we both ordered coffee, and Ruby ordered a Derbyshire oatcake with cheese and bacon.

'I still haven't had lunch,' she said, shaking her head. 'We had some problems with the ticketing system, so I've spent most of the day trying to fix that.'

I took in my surroundings: this was a real tearoom, not a café. It was formed of multiple rooms, the warm yellow walls displaying black and white drawings in gold frames. We sat on high-backed wicker chairs around a table with white crockery and a small white vase holding delicate white flowers. Simple brass chandeliers hung from decorative ceiling roses. It was easy to imagine a Jane Austen character walking in and taking a seat.

'I was so excited when you called. Tina has told me all about the murders you've been involved in.' I didn't like the idea that I was 'involved' in any murder, but I knew what she meant. 'How can I help?'

I glanced around the room. 'Is there likely to be anyone from the Festival in here?'

'No, I checked the diaries. Everyone is either out visiting sites or they're upstairs, and anyway, I'd recognise anyone who was, so we're safe.' Tina had told me I could trust her sister, and I trusted Tina's opinion on everything except haggis, which she described as the food of the devil, so I felt comfortable being completely open with Ruby.

'I want to find out more about Arianna and her brother, Maxwell. How involved is he?'

'In the Festival? Officially, not at all. He's a donor, but that's it. He's more interested in sport. His company is a major sponsor of a local football team and he funds a summer football training school for youths under fifteen. Unofficially, I guess you'd call him an advisor to his sister. More recently, he's been increasingly dropping by to see her. I manage her diary and they've had lunch together quite a lot.'

A server in a frilly white shirt and little black apron came with our drinks: a cafetière for two and white china cups and saucers.

'Have you ever heard them talk about the theatre at Charleton House?'

'The *Romeo and Juliet* production?'

'No, the plan to renovate and reopen the 19th-century theatre. It's a pet project of the Duchess's.'

'Oh, that. Yes, actually. You'd think it was part of the Festival, although it won't be until next year. Right now, they're two very separate projects and it's nothing to do with us.'

'But Arianna and her brother talk about it like it is?'

Ruby nodded as she poured us both a cup of coffee. 'Sugar?' I shook my head. 'I know that Maxwell thinks she should direct the opening play, he's made that very clear and talks about it quite openly. Arianna is a bit more cagey about it, but I know she's interested and I would guess she's a sure bet now.'

I assumed from the way Ruby phrased her comment that Arianna's appointment wasn't public knowledge.

'How does he go about it? I mean, is he quite aggressive in the way he wants her to get the job? If he's not interested in the arts, why does he bother?'

She shrugged. 'He's the caring, if slightly domineering brother who wants to see his younger sister succeed. I wouldn't call him aggressive, but he has clear ideas and I don't think he's used to not getting what he wants. He was very successful in business early on and he bankrolled some of Arianna's first projects. He's also encouraged her to try and get some more publicity, put herself in the limelight a bit more.'

'How far do you think he'd go to make sure she got the job of directing the opening play at Charleton?'

Ruby put her cup back in its saucer and leaned towards me, lowering her voice as she said, 'Are you asking me if he'd kill Miranda so Arianna could get the job?' I nodded. 'Honestly, I have no idea. He's always been nice enough to me – although I have heard him bark instructions down the phone to his staff – but like I say, he's incredibly successful and I don't think he's *ever* experienced failure. I've no idea what he'd do if it did happen to him.'

We quickly stopped talking as Ruby's lunch was delivered. The oatcake, which looked like a thick pancake, was folded in half and stuffed with melted cheese and strips of bacon. We occasionally served them in the Garden Café with a salad; the texture always reminded me of a thin crumpet.

Once the server was far enough away, Ruby leaned over the table again. 'Tell me what it's like, solving murders.' She tucked into her oatcake, her eyes flicking back to me, waiting for me to speak. I wasn't sure it was a question I could answer, or at least, I doubted I could give her the deep philosophical response she was most likely looking for.

'Satisfying, a relief once the murderer has been caught. It's hard to describe. I'm just so glad when it's all over that I'm pleased to get on with more mundane things. It's not something I look forward to – someone has died and I'd much rather they hadn't.'

'Of course, but still, it must be exciting?'

I didn't have the heart to talk further about my mixed feelings and how tricky it could be navigating anything that was linked to the Duke and Duchess, so I gave her an easy answer.

'Yes, very. I wouldn't want to make a career of it, but it certainly livens things up.'

She grinned at me. 'Well, if you ever need any help, give me a call. I think it would be fascinating.'

I watched as she finished off the oatcake, wondering how much help she had given me today. I wasn't convinced she had described Maxwell as someone who would destroy anything that got between him and success, but if, as Ruby said, he wasn't used to failure, and it involved a family member he was close to, then perhaps fear of the job going to Miranda might have made him snap. And now I thought about it, I recalled him re-entering the Long Gallery shortly before I had found Miranda's body. I had no idea how long he had been away from the party, but it could easily have been long enough to find and kill Miranda. The Duchess had reassured Arianna that she had yet to make a decision when Miranda had died, but at the time, it was clearly getting close to the wire – too close for Maxwell's comfort?

After Ruby had finished eating, she told me a bit more about the way the Festival was managed. Then we prepared to leave and I thanked her for her time. The only other person I could think of who would possibly be able to tell me how Maxwell's ambitions might play out was the Duchess. But it was going to take me a while to develop the courage to do that.

It was time to head home, get a good night's sleep and prepare myself for a difficult conversation.

CHAPTER 17

'Sophie... Sophie... Anyone home?'

Tina was waving her hand in front of me.

'The café is open and you have a visitor. I've also made you a coffee, it's on the counter. You look like you need another.'

I had a mirror in my desk drawer, but after that comment, I decided it might be best not to look in it, regardless of who was out there waiting for me. There wasn't much I could do to rectify the situation. My mother used to say I always looked like I'd been blown into the room by a strong wind, and nothing had changed.

I came out to find DS Harnby paying for her black filter coffee. She was a stickler for the rules and wouldn't even accept a free coffee from me.

'Sophie, join me. I've just finished confirming a few things with your Head of Security and have half an hour before I need to be anywhere.'

'Anything interesting? From Security, I mean?'

She peered at me over her mug. It was easy to imagine a suspect quickly becoming very uncomfortable on the receiving end of one of her stares.

I shrugged. 'It was worth a try.'

'It was. But you must realise that I have my Sophie shield switched on whenever I'm near you.' She used her mug-free hand to mime a force field coming down in front of her. 'Try as you might, I'm not going to let anything slip, unless it's part of my plan. You, on the other hand, need to tell me everything you know.'

'What makes you think I know anything?' I said, trying to sound confused.

'Give it a rest, Sophie. I'm sure you ask questions in your sleep, and if you're not doing that, you'll be earwigging on conversations in here.'

'Hey, I'm too busy to earwig.'

'Hmmm,' was the only reply I got to that. I liked Harnby so figured I'd tell her what I knew, or most of it. I wanted to keep one thing under my hat until I'd had a chance to find out more.

'You know that both Miranda Summerscale and Arianna Mountford were being considered for the role of director of the first play to be staged when the Charleton House theatre is reopened?'

'Yes, I do.'

'You know that her brother was highly ambitious on her behalf?'

'Mmm, makes sense, but being a supportive sibling is one thing, killing in order to get your sister a job is a whole different thing. What else have you got?'

'You know that Miranda was making life difficult for her ex-husband and his girlfriend and they are both working on the production?'

'Yes and yes. I also know that about ten other people had the opportunity to kill Miranda in circumstances that mean they wouldn't necessarily be missed for the short time it took to strangle her.'

'Okay. See, I'm not digging around and finding out anything new.'

'Clearly. I'm surprised, Sophie, even a little disappointed.'

'So, if I had found out something useful, you'd tell me off for snooping, and now I haven't, you're disappointed?'

'Something like that.' She paused. 'Tell me more about Ariana's brother.'

'Ahh, so you didn't know about that.'

'Just tell me what you know.'

I filled her in on his unusually large donation and his encouragement of his sister.

'Okay, I'll admit we didn't know about the donation. It doesn't seem particularly strange that he would give a bigger donation to a project that his sister was involved with, or had the potential to be involved with. It might raise a few eyebrows, but having a supportive family member is a positive thing. I will take a look at it, though. Anything else you want to contribute?'

'No, nothing.'

'That's not entirely true – you also neglected to tell me that a member of the cast has been paying you a lot of attention.'

'Who? Richard? Oh, please! I get attention off a lot of the cast, they all come into the café, it would be rude for them to ignore me.' Harnby didn't look convinced. I wasn't sure I'd convinced myself, either; I still felt a warm glow when I thought about him working in Leeds.

She looked at me, waiting for me to continue.

'Okay, so I like him. But I'm not in any rush. I left one disastrous relationship back in London, I'm in no hurry to make the same mistake again.'

'What hurry? You've been here two years.' She had a point.

'Why are you interested? Is he a suspect?'

'No, he's not, but if you do start spending more time with him, I hope for his sake you're not just using the poor guy to get information.'

I wasn't aware I'd been doing anything of the kind; I genuinely enjoyed his company.

'What do you take me for?' I knew I'd stretched the boundaries of the law a few times, but I wasn't about to lead someone on like that. If I happened to get any useful information from him during some of our conversations, then so be it.

Harnby smiled at me. 'I don't actually think you'd do that. But whatever happens, let me know. I'm always the last to hear the latest gossip back at the station.'

'I'm surprised you're the type.'

She'd softened towards me over the months, but still, I viewed her as the hard-nosed, ambitious type.

'What type? Human?'

'No, just...'

'I'm kidding, but you can probably imagine what it's like. I have to keep my nose to the grindstone. If the fellas chat about other people's relationships, or who's good-looking, it's banter. If I do it, it's gossip and I'm just a distracted woman who can't concentrate on the job.' A resigned smile appeared on her lips. 'It's getting better for women in the force, slowly. In the meantime, let me know how it goes.'

She stood up and pulled her jacket on, the steel grey fabric of her suit forming the perfect costume for the role she had to play. As she left, I pondered over how hard a job the police had trying to narrow the suspects down. I had intentionally kept Ginger's name out of the conversation, which was perhaps a little unfair, but hey, Harnby must know tons that I had no clue about. I was also worried about Joyce if we found out that Ginger was in some way involved. If that was the case, I wanted to have some control over her discovery of the information. And I still believed that Joyce might have a better chance than anyone of extracting information from her newfound friend.

I remained at the table after Harnby had left, mulling over everything I knew, but my coffee mug was empty and I still wasn't firing on all cylinders. It was time to bite the bullet and visit Ginger. The more I thought about it, the less convinced I was that she was the innocent landlady who just happened to have Miranda staying with her.

'Sophie.' Richard was smiling down on me. 'Can I get you another?' The man had impeccable timing, I'd give him that. A couple of minutes later, he was seated opposite me. His hair was a soft brown with flecks of silver and looked as if he'd done no more than run his fingers through it when he got up. What was it with men? Joe was just the same. Mind you, it made me feel less awkward about the possible state of my own hair this morning. We could be windswept together.

'I hope you don't mind me asking, but what do you remember of the fire at the Castledale School?'

A shadow crossed over his face and I wondered if I'd dug too deep too quickly. He sighed.

'I'm sorry, I didn't mean to...'

'No, don't apologise. It's fine. It was a long time ago, although coming back to Derbyshire for the Festival has brought a lot of memories back. In some respects, there's not a lot to tell. We had just finished a rehearsal. *A Midsummer Night's Dream*. We left – well, most of us – and went home. The next thing is I get a phone call from a school friend telling me the school is on fire. We went and sat on a hill that overlooked the school and watched the theatre block burn. It wasn't until the next day that we heard someone had died.'

'Did you know Leo Salt?'

'No more than the other pupils. He always seemed really nice and was happy to stay behind and help out. A year later, they had rebuilt the theatre and surrounding buildings. They put a courtyard in the middle which holds the memorial garden for Leo. It was very thoughtful.'

'You must have made a lot of use of the new theatre.'

He shook his head. 'Not me. I didn't go back to do my A-Levels there. I was due to start at a college the next town over. Castledale had a theatre, but it didn't have an actual drama department. The college did, and all the time I spent working on plays with Miranda had really cemented my desire to go to drama school, so I decided I would be better off on that course. Added to which, my dad was the headmaster at Castledale and the idea of not running into him in the corridor every day was very appealing. Being at the same school could make things quite challenging for us, and we didn't have a great relationship at the best of times.'

I had some understanding of this. My mum had been a maths teacher, but luckily at a different school to the one I went to. It was lucky for her as much as me – I hadn't inherited her head for figures, and I would probably have been a huge embarrassment. But she did insist on extra maths lessons at home, which I rebelled against, to no avail. To this day, she often expresses her incredulity that I have done as well as I have in my career when it is almost necessary for me to remove my socks to count beyond ten. I'd quickly learnt the importance of building very strong relationships with accountants and finance staff, which currently included turning up with pastries whenever my expenses forms were due in.

'But what about Miranda? Didn't she want to do the same and study drama?'

'Not that I'm aware of, and certainly once she saw the plans for the new theatre, she didn't want to go anywhere else. It was state of the art.'

'I believe they never caught the person who started the fire.'

He shook his head. 'No, although there were thoughts that it was some local kids. A village hall had gone up in smoke some weeks earlier, so the police thought that was kids mucking about who had then chanced their arms and started the fire at the school. That was the last one. If it was kids, then I'm sure they never intended to hurt anyone and they've been carrying the guilt round with them ever since. Do you think it might be related to Miranda's death?'

I paused, wondering how much I should share with him, but Harnby had said he wasn't a suspect and I had a good feeling about him. I knew I should probably give those feelings a little more thought, but I didn't have any concerns, so I decided to take the chance.

'I can't see how, but it does raise some questions about Ginger.'

'You think she might be avenging her brother's death? But that would have to mean she felt that Miranda was at fault, and yet she was nearly a victim herself.'

He had a point.

'True, but some people can lay the blame in strange places as they deal with their grief.'

'You seem rather interested in all of this. Do you watch a lot of *CSI*? Read a lot of Agatha Christie?'

I laughed. 'I have a bit of a reputation as an amateur sleuth, I'll admit. It's interesting, and oddly addictive once you get started.'

'So, you're the village Sherlock? I'd better watch what I say, or do; you're probably examining my every move.'

I didn't take offence; there was nothing but gentle amusement in his face. I enjoyed a bit of teasing and I was pretty sure he could take it as well as hand it out.

'So, Sherlock, or should I call you Miss Marple? Who else has appeared under your magnifying glass?'

I felt bad about saying too much – these were his friends, so I shook my head.

'I don't have many ideas, I'm just knocking things around.'

'Well, I'll be sure to behave myself. Something tells me I wouldn't be able to get much past you.' He winked as he gathered up his things. 'See you later, Sherlock.'

CHAPTER 18

Joyce was furious. Actually, it was worse than that.

When I'd asked her if she fancied going for a drive to see Ginger, she had leapt at the chance. As we walked towards the car, I'd told her my suspicions and immediately regretted it. Having Joyce at the wheel of a car is hair-raising at the best of times – there's always a chance I'm going to get out of the passenger seat with whiplash, having had my ears chewed off with a string of profanities. What I got instead was one of the creepiest journeys I'd ever experienced.

Joyce remained silent, the warmth of the sun seeming to be propelled from the car's interior by the strength of her mood. She hadn't lowered the roof, which was completely out of character, and she followed the speed limit religiously. If I didn't know better, I would have believed that she was quietly plotting murder – *my* murder.

I didn't notice the scenery; I was too busy wondering if Ginger really could be involved. If I got this wrong, I was risking not only offending Ginger, but my friendship with Joyce.

We slowly crawled to a stop outside Ginger's house and she appeared at the front door with a tray of drinks. I'd called her to let her know we were on our way and she'd sounded over the moon.

'This is a nice surprise, I hadn't expected to see either of you today. Although in that outfit, Joyce dear, you've probably been spotted by any astronauts circling overhead.'

Joyce was wearing a yellow leather motorcycle jacket, under which was a loose silk shirt with a geometric pattern made up of blue, yellow and purple triangles. She'd painted her nails to match the jacket, but the end result looked as though she'd dipped her fingers in mustard.

'Now then,' continued Ginger, 'I know it's always cocktail hour somewhere in the world, but I think we should pretend to have some decorum. Sophie, I've been filled in on just how much of a coffee fiend you are. Joyce... well, you gave up any pretence of decorum years ago, so I pulled out this little bottle of wine I found in the back of the fridge. We drank everything else the other night.' She examined the label of the bottle with a look of distaste. 'Probably tastes like vinegar, but it's cold and wet.'

I expected Joyce to put on some show of hurt feelings or disgust, but as we walked through the gate, I heard her chortle.

'Didn't take you long to get the measure of me, Ginger Salt. It's no wonder we get on.' I couldn't help but notice that Joyce, who always worked hard to sound like the lady of the manor, had already started dropping the occasional consonant in Ginger's company.

Ginger was staring at the car. 'I've been thinking, you should take me out for a spin in that – with the top down. We could take a few trips over the summer.'

'Anytime, Ginger, just say the word. We'll be Derbyshire's answer to Thelma and Louise.'

Ginger sniggered. 'So long as I get to live happily ever after with Brad Pitt.' They both laughed and Ginger handed Joyce a glass of liquid resembling something that ought to be tested in a lab.

'Now then, I know you girls are on a mission.'

'Well, *she* is.' Joyce's voice dropped an octave and the cold stare returned as she looked my way. 'And I want to make it very clear, Ginger dear, that I feel offended on your behalf and apologise in advance for...'

'Do be quiet, Joyce. I'm very difficult to offend – as you well know after your less than delicate comments about my dress sense the other night. Whatever Sophie has to say, she is welcome to say it. Now, Sophie, spit it out. I guess this is something to do with Miranda.'

I took a sip of coffee and tried not to make too much noise as I placed the cup back on its saucer. I knew two sets of eyes were boring into me and I felt very much under the spotlight.

'I'm sorry to raise this, Ginger, but I'm aware you had a brother, and I believe he died in the fire at the school Miranda went to.'

The smile left Ginger's face, but it was replaced with a softness, not anger.

'That's right, Leo. He was my older brother and he'd grown to be a good man. He was the caretaker, and yes, he died trying to fight the fire. After he'd alerted Miranda and her friends and got them out, he went back in and tried to put it out. The fire got the better of him.'

'I'm so sorry. You must miss him.'

'Oh, I do, every day. But he would have wanted me to crack on with life and told me to stop being so soppy.' Joyce rested her hand on Ginger's arm. Ginger patted her hand in return. 'What else is on your mind, Sophie? That can't be it.'

Joyce glared at me, daring me to continue.

'Do you blame Miranda for his death?'

Joyce let out a huff and turned away from me.

'It's alright, Joyce, the girl can ask me anything she wants. Now drink your wine and relax. You'll give yourself an aneurysm.'

Joyce harrumphed and downed the rest of the wine in one gulp.

'Do I blame Miranda? I won't deny there was a time when I did. I needed to blame someone, and over the years, I've blamed everyone with even the most tenuous link to what happened. If Miranda hadn't wanted to stay late with some of the cast, Leo would never have been there when the fire started. Of course, that's ridiculous, I know that now.'

'But isn't it a little strange that you'd invite her to stay with you during the Shakespeare Festival?'

'I didn't. Well, not exactly. The Festival has a directory of accommodation. It gets sent to theatre companies, and if they have company members who need somewhere to stay, they can take a look at the directory, find somewhere suitable and give the hosts a call. I'm in that directory.'

'Quite a coincidence, though, isn't it?'

'Not really. I'm the only one on the list here in Castledale. This is where Miranda grew up and we're only fifteen minutes from Charleton House. It makes sense that she might want to "come home", so to speak.'

'I told you, Sophie, I said you were being ridiculous.' Joyce sat up straight as she spoke, vindication in every word.

'It's alright, you told me yourself about her Miss Marple tendencies. It makes perfect sense that she'd want to ask a few questions. Sophie, I don't know what I expected to feel when she arrived; the last time I saw her in the flesh was at the dedication of Leo's memorial garden. After that, it was the occasional photo in the newspaper. She's thirty years older now... sorry, was. A different person.'

'But wouldn't she have recognised your name when she booked? I'm surprised it didn't put her off,' Joyce asked. I loved that despite her annoyance at me and her loyalty to Ginger, Joyce had let her curiosity get the better of her.

'It wasn't actually Miranda who called. She had an assistant.'

'And you didn't talk about the fire while she was here?' I found it hard to believe that even the most British hyper-politeness could have prevented the conversation turning to that awful event for too long.

'Eventually, yes, briefly. She was very good, didn't linger on it for too long. I'm sure she thought it would be too painful for me.'

'Sophie,' Joyce looked at me, a serious although slightly less angry expression on her face, 'do you have any more questions?'

'One more,' I replied. She tutted. 'Ginger, you were at Charleton House the night that Miranda died. Wasn't Miranda going to the pub with the others after the reception?'

'Oh no, she liked to keep things separate. She'd go once or twice, show willing, then she'd leave them to it. It was far enough along in rehearsals that she was no longer joining them, so I agreed to collect her when the reception was due to end at nine o'clock.'

'It was good of you to drive her about so much.'

'It was no bother; I'm largely retired and have a lot of time on my hands.'

'Did you...'

'Sophie, that's enough! You've had your *one more.*' Ginger was fine with the questions, but I'd clearly tested Joyce's patience.

'Thank you, Ginger, I appreciate it.'

'You're quite alright. Ignore Miss Mardypants.'

'Do you mind if I use your bathroom?'

'Go right ahead. There's one downstairs, just past the bottom of the staircase.'

I left the two women debating the appropriateness of Joyce's new nickname and went inside. The toilet was, as Ginger had said, towards the end of a narrow hallway, but first I couldn't resist the urge to stick my head around the door into the sitting room. It was a homely space with a big comfy sofa. Knitting had been left on the armchair facing the television. The double doors that led to the dining room were open, revealing a large table that held a sewing machine and all sorts of pieces of fabric. A wooden box sat open, spools of thread spilling out.

A bookcase held a fantastic collection of murder mystery books. They had been displayed so that interspersed between the books were small ornaments and framed photos. It was a warm, welcoming space, but something was missing.

I took a closer look at the bookcase and the photos of, I assumed, family and friends. There was not a single photo of anyone who could have been Leo, her – apparently – much-loved brother.

CHAPTER 19

I was keen to fill Mark in with my additional concerns. I hadn't discussed the lack of photos with Joyce; it was all becoming far too sensitive, and during our rather quiet journey back to the house, I had decided that it was better I didn't share my continuing suspicions.

As Joyce and I parted ways outside one of the gift shops, she simply looked at me and said firmly, 'She didn't do it,' and then marched off, her heels clacking loudly on the stone steps. As least her staff had a heads-up that she was back.

Mark, on the other hand, was positively beaming as he ran across the courtyard towards me.

'Soph, Soph, we've got permission to start preparing a new tour on the… what's up? You don't look too cheerful.' I looked back at the entrance to the shop through which Joyce had disappeared. 'Oh dear, have you poked the dragon?'

'Apparently so. But I guess that was bound to happen when I started pointing a finger at her new best friend.'

'You still think Ginger might be involved?' I nodded, filling him in while watching the Duchess and a smartly dressed woman walk into the courtyard, deep in conversation.

'I don't know what it all means, and I'm really hard pressed to imagine her killing Miranda. I agree with Joyce inasmuch as I just don't get the feeling Ginger could do something like that, but the photos…'

'Yeah, and plenty of serial killers who charmed their way into their victims' lives were people you would never suspect.'

'Mark, do you have a moment?' The Duchess walked towards us. Even on cobbles, she maintained her dignified, graceful walk. 'I'm sorry to disturb you both; it's just that I think you might be able to help me with a small problem, Mark.'

'Tell me how I can help.' Despite being a man who declared that not only was he at the gay end of the spectrum of sexualities, he fell right off it, Mark practically melted in the presence of the Duchess. If she'd asked him to run laps around the estate, naked, in the dead of winter, I was sure he'd strip off there and then and set off into an icy wind without a moment's hesitation.

'I know you've appeared on camera before, would you be prepared to do it again?'

'Absolutely.'

'I realise it's short notice: a regional news show wants to do a feature about the Festival and they'd like to do it here with the house as a backdrop. They've asked if someone could talk about Charleton a little and I'm sure you could find a few theatrical references to throw in.'

'It would be my pleasure.' He gave the front of his waistcoat a little tug and pulled his shoulders back.

'Wonderful, thank you, Mark. There's just one other thing…'

She rested her arm lightly on his and steered him towards the woman who had been waiting on the other side of the courtyard. I didn't hear the rest of the conversation; I was still distracted by thoughts of Ginger, and besides which, it was time I actually went and did some work before my team started managing upwards and decided to find some way to fire me.

. . .

WITH JOYCE OUT of the way and Mark on a mission for the Duchess, I pulled out my mobile phone as I walked back to the café and called Ruby at the Festival office. She was pleased to hear from me and excited at the prospect of helping me out again.

'Do you have anything to do with the housing list?' I asked. 'Helping actors find accommodation?'

'Sometimes. We're a small team and we all muck in. What are you looking for?'

'I believe the list is sent out to theatre companies, and then it's over to them to go through it and call the homeowner.'

'Mmm,' Ruby agreed.

'Do you ever have a homeowner making a particular request? Maybe they only want a female lodger?'

'That does happen, but we always put that kind of criteria next to their details on the list. A gender-specific request isn't uncommon; most of them say no smoking, a couple say no alcohol in the house, but that's not very common. They also say if they've got pets in case the person enquiring has allergies.'

I reminded myself that Tina had assured me I could trust her sister, so I gave her Ginger's name. 'Is there any way that she might have requested someone from the *Romeo and Juliet* company, or maybe even Miranda specifically? She knew that Miranda didn't have family here anymore so would have needed somewhere to stay. Could she have done anything to engineer having Miranda stay with her?'

I heard the sound of furious typing on a keyboard.

'Let me have a look at the database, we would have recorded any special requests. Okay, Ginger was new to us. She signed up about four months ago, so she hadn't done this before, and yes, there is a note saying that she would prefer to have her details offered to the *Romeo and Juliet* company, and had requested a female lodger only.'

'Does it say why she made that request?'

'No, but the Festival is getting bigger every year and we've been trying to build the list, so we're grateful to people who put their names forward whatever the limitations.'

'Thanks, Ruby, you're a star.'

'Anytime – let me know if I can do anything else for you.' I promised I would and hung up.

So Ginger hadn't gone as far as specifically requesting Miranda, and from the way the housing list worked, that wouldn't have been easy to engineer. But she had increased the chances of it being Miranda, and if not Miranda, then a member of the cast who might have been able to give her information about or even access to their director.

Ginger wasn't being entirely honest with us.

I WAS TRYING to perfect a rustic cinnamon bun which a number of staff had requested I introduce to the menu. I'm not a professional pastry chef – just the mere suggestion of that would cause guffaws of laughter to come from almost everyone who knows me – but I enjoy baking and the pastry chef who works with me is happy to teach me a few things. I have reached the point where I can help out with a few of our commonly baked cakes and pastries, and I am rather proud of my croissants, a notoriously difficult bake to do well. I also find baking to be a good distraction: it frees up my mind, which often leads to a few 'aha' moments, and it makes me look like I am working – albeit not at something I am actually paid to do.

I had just pulled the buns out of the oven and was wondering how soon I could risk burning my tongue to try one when Tina came running into the kitchen. This in itself was an event. Tina is never flustered, never stressed, and I have never seen her run, but she came crashing through the doors with a very mischievous grin on her face.

'Sophie, you have to come, quick. And bring your phone, you're going to want pictures of this.'

Tina dragged me by the arm into the courtyard. Joyce was already there, watching a camera crew setting up. I spotted Mark's head in the midst of a small group of people, one of whom seemed to be dabbing his forehead with makeup.

Joyce grinned. 'This might be the best day of my life.' I knew better than to think that I had been forgiven, but something had certainly lightened her mood, and it wasn't long until I found out what it was.

As the crew stepped back, Mark... or, should I say, William Shakespeare was revealed. He was dressed in a burgundy doublet, the sleeves swollen just beyond the shoulder, making him look as though he possessed a rather oddly shaped pair of biceps. His short breeches stopped at the top of his thighs – they must have been padded because they looked as if they were hiding a pair of marrows rather than normally shaped legs. The eye then carried on down his legs, taking in the tights. Mark had legs so skinny they resembled a pair of pipe cleaners, and the tights only exaggerated this. He looked as if he might snap at the first gust of wind.

But it wasn't his legs that had caught Joyce's eye. 'My, my, you could keep your phone *and* keys in that.' She made no attempt to hide what she was staring at with a rather louche look on her face. Mark was wearing a magnificent codpiece in matching burgundy and decorated with a line of pearls. 'Careful,' she added, 'you might get done under the Trades Description Act.'

Mark pursed his lips and narrowed his eyes. 'You finished yet?'

'Oh no, I'm going to be dining out on this for a long time to come.' She looked him up and down again, and then added, 'Those heels are higher than mine. I've got a pair of Jimmy Choo's you might like. They'd actually look great with one of your suits. I have a sky-blue pair that would really pop with your navy pinstripe.'

He looked at me with an expression of desperation. 'Apparently, it was the moustache that gave them the idea. Remind me to chop it off the minute this is over. I did suggest one of the live interpretation team – we do have a Shakespeare on site, but it seems he's booked to deliver some education sessions this afternoon. Quite how I'm meant to be taken seriously looking like this, I don't know, and it's going out live.'

'Never fear, my dear,' declared Joyce, 'I don't think I've taken you seriously since the day I first clapped eyes on you, so you have nothing to lose. You'll be inundated with calls asking if you do strippergrams and you'll be bursting out of grannies' birthday cakes in no time. I bet you could double your current salary if you took this on as a side job.'

Mark stormed off, almost tripping on a cobble. He glanced back, looking as furious as a man in tights can, while the three of us howled with laughter.

CHAPTER 20

'The director wanted me to keep twirling my moustache. I was Shakespeare, not some villain in a Victorian melodrama, and that bloody codpiece! They were no longer in fashion when Shakespeare came along.'

Mark was grumbling into a mug of coffee. 'I did tell them, but the director liked the way it looked. If I'm going to look ridiculous, my outfit should at least be historically accurate.'

'I thought you looked fabulous, and be honest, you quite like being in front of the camera.'

There was a pause, and then he peered up at me. 'Yeah, alright, I do rather. I was dropping hints about how it had been a while since there had been a documentary about Charleton House. They could do a behind the scenes, with a whole episode about the tours.'

'Chances are they'd skirt over you and Joyce would be centre stage. She's certainly colourful enough, I bet the cameras would love her, *daarling*,' I ended on a flourish. Mark lost his smile.

'You're probably right. Bad idea. Is Lady Macbeth talking to you again, or do you remain firmly in her bad books?'

'She's talking to me, but I don't think I'm in her top ten of favourite people. I have my work cut out there.'

Mark was using a paper napkin to remove the remaining makeup from his face. 'Do you really think Ginger might have killed Miranda? You need to be pretty sure if you're going to risk your friendship with Joyce.'

'It's not that bad – she's annoyed, but I know she's curious. She's probably holed up in her office stressing about it right now. But I really don't know. Something's not right, though; either Ginger has never had photos of her brother on display, which seems odd when there are plenty of photos of other people and he is apparently a much-loved and missed family member, or she's removed them.'

'Why would she do that?' he asked as I took the napkin from him and rubbed another streak of makeup off. I was surprised he let me and attacked a smudge on his neck while I had the chance.

'There must be some reason she didn't want Miranda to know who she was, that she knew about the fire or had any connection to it, certainly in the beginning. Ginger said they had eventually discussed it, but only briefly. That doesn't quite add up to me; I'm sure she was up to something, but I don't know what.'

'I'm surprised Miranda didn't recognise Ginger's surname from the start. That was a traumatic event for her, too, so she was bound to remember Leo's name. Ginger must have accepted there was a very strong chance Miranda would put two and two together and realise who she was.'

'True; perhaps she felt it was a risk worth taking, that this was an opportunity to try and find out more that she just couldn't ignore. She did what she could to limit the chances of that happening, but was equally prepared for Miranda to realise straight away.'

'Do you think Joyce might be able to help you figure it out?'

I shook my head. 'In her eyes, Ginger can do no wrong. Joyce clearly adored her sister, and since her death, I imagine she's taken on even more of a saint-like status. I don't mean that to sound harsh, but any rough edges her sister had will have been smoothed over with time. If Ginger really reminds her of Bunny, then she's taken on the same saintly status – for now, anyway. Hopefully the friendship will develop a more grounded footing over time. Right now, though, Joyce has a new-friend crush and is neither use nor ornament when it comes to Ginger. This is something I need to figure out on my own.'

Mark picked up his phone and notebook and got ready to leave. I nodded towards the items in his hand.

'You should have asked to keep the codpiece, it could have been useful.'

'Nah, it was too small, I need to order an extra-large.' He winked at me.

As Mark left, I noticed how quiet the café was and looked at my watch. It was six o'clock. We'd been so deep in conversation, I hadn't noticed the café close. The doors were locked, the tables had been cleared and wiped down, the children's highchairs were neatly stacked in the corner and only two members of staff remained to empty the till.

There was something I needed to do. It was a risk, but it was one angle on the murder that I hadn't dug deeply enough into.

AFTER CHECKING with her rather intimidating guard dog of an assistant, I knew that the Duchess had returned to the theatre and I decided to try to have a chat with her there. I pushed open the door, stopping as I remembered I hadn't put on a hard hat and grabbing one before continuing. Stepping into the gloom of the auditorium, I let my eyes adjust. A figure was walking down the far side of the seats; I recognised the Duchess immediately and made my way over, my stomach churning.

She turned quickly as I neared.

'Oh! Sophie, you took me by surprise. I'm just fetching some swatches I left behind. I've decided that we should reupholster the seats. They're not in bad condition, but I want to do this properly.' She removed the dustsheet from the first two seats on the end of a row, showing me the deep red fabric. They looked fine to me. 'What are you doing here?'

'I was actually looking for you.'

'Well, you've found me. How can I help? Come, let's have a seat.' I followed her down a few more rows to seats that weren't underneath the balcony. Here it wasn't so dark and I could see her face more clearly. She pulled back another dustsheet and took a seat. I sat next to her. I paused for a moment, wondering how to start, but she spoke first.

'I remember the first time I saw this theatre like it was yesterday: it was the night I met my husband – well, husband-to-be.' She looked at me and smiled. As far as it was possible to tell, she and the Duke were very happily married, so it was no surprise that her memory would return to that day with such ease. 'Believe it or not, I was actually here to spend time with his brother. I'd met Charles in London and we were rather taken with each other. As I was due to be in Derbyshire visiting friends, he'd invited me over to see a production of *The Importance of Being Earnest* they were staging.

'Some of the family were performing, along with a few members of staff. Charles was playing Lady Bracknell and was very funny – he has superb comedic timing. But things became a little more dramatic than he had intended when I met his older brother, Alexander. I have no idea how serious Charles was about me, but he later said that as soon as he saw the expression on Alexander's face, he knew he had lost me. They didn't talk to one another until the morning of our wedding, a year later.'

She paused, staring off into the distance.

'Do they get on well now?'

'Oh yes, thick as thieves. Alexander was best man at Charles's wedding. Of course, the story gets rolled out at family gatherings and Charles now takes full credit for our marriage, the existence of our children, most of our business decisions: *"If I hadn't brought Evelyn to Charleton, you would never have met and such and such would never have occurred".* I have threatened to put *"If I hadn't brought Evelyn to Charleton..."* on his headstone. But I doubt my marriage is what you wanted to talk to me about, so how can I help?'

My throat suddenly felt very dry and my stomach hollow. My first few words came out as raspy and uncertain, but I kept going.

'I was struck by something in the list of sponsors for *Romeo and Juliet* and the theatre renovation. Maxwell Mountford has donated quite a substantial amount, more than he typically gives. Yet, I'm aware that he has no real interest in theatre, except...' I stopped, regretting my decision to talk to the Duchess. 'Except for his sister.'

'Yes, he has been extremely generous. It's one of the reasons I feel I can consider reupholstering all of the seats.'

'I was just wondering, have you spoken to him about it at all? Did he say anything about why he wanted to give more this time?' I watched as uncertainty crossed her face; she clearly wondered where I was going with this line of questioning.

'I have met him, a number of times.'

'I'm just wondering if, perhaps, he thought...'

'...that if he donated a large sum of money, I would in return give his sister the role of director for the opening production? Is this where you are heading with this, Sophie? Are you really of the opinion that I could be, shall we say, convinced to make certain decisions as a result of a financial investment in Charleton House?'

The coolness in her voice made me think of a slab of cold stone and I wished the seat could swallow me up.

'No, I don't think you could... at all... I just... I've just been trying to think of who could have something to gain from

Miranda's death and if Maxwell had tried that angle, but it hadn't worked...'

'If that was his motivation, then no, it most definitely wouldn't have worked. I hadn't made my final decision when Miranda was so tragically murdered. Look, Sophie,' she sighed and her voice softened a little, 'my husband and I have turned a blind eye to you becoming so involved in many of the dramatic events that have occurred in recent years. It wouldn't be unfair to say that our silence has probably encouraged you, and between you and me, the Duke has attempted to defend you from concerns that senior police officers have communicated to us.' I knew she meant Detective Inspector Mike Flynn, Harnby's boss, who had made it very clear that he didn't like me. But he seemed to spend a lot of time toadying up to the Duke, so it was no surprise to me that if the Duke had defended me, DI Flynn had listened. 'But you need to be very careful not to get too involved and neglect your work. You are an employee, an excellent employee, and I don't want to see you put your work at risk, or put yourself in danger, if it were to come to that.'

I wondered if my heart was ever going to start beating again – I had expected a strong telling off. After an interminably long silence, the Duchess slowly turned to face me.

'I did wonder about the size of the donation, but Maxwell has given a great deal of money over the years. I also recognise that he's much more interested in football stadiums than theatres. But at the time, I already knew that Miranda was in the stronger position for the role. I hadn't made up my mind for certain, but I was increasingly leaning towards her. Maxwell has never said anything directly; he's made a few comments about how much his sister could bring to the job, but I always changed the subject when that happened. I *have* been concerned about how this might look to others. But what's done is done. It will teach me to be much more circumspect in the future.'

The Duchess stood up to leave. 'Do you think he might have been prepared to go that far to ensure his sister was appointed?'

I wasn't sure I'd heard her right. 'I'm sorry?'

'Maxwell, do you believe he might have killed Miranda?'

'I don't know, but he does seem to be very used to getting everything he wants. Do you think he might be capable of it?'

'I'm not in the habit of accusing people of murder, I'll leave that to you. But I've never felt very comfortable around him.'

Silence descended again and I took that as my cue to leave.

I PLACED mugs in front of Joe and DS Harnby and pulled up a seat. My staff had long gone and we'd had to take chairs from the tables in order to sit down.

'How did she react to your inappropriate line of questioning?' Harnby asked with a stern look on her face. It seemed that the mortification I felt for talking to the Duchess about Maxwell was clearly written across my expression and Harnby had asked if everything was alright. I'd decided to come clean with them both and asked them if they wanted a drink in the silent café. Joe was flicking through a Japanese translation of *Richard III* that he'd removed from a shelf.

'I wish I'd been a fly on the wall, you're lucky she didn't hand you your P45,' was his contribution.

'I know.' I sighed. 'I was lucky she took it so well. I'm not sure I'll take that chance again.'

'Again!' Harnby exclaimed. 'How about never? How about actually doing as we tell you and leaving all this to the professionals? If you have some information, you call us, do you hear? You call us, instead of putting your job at risk and possibly giving me a reason to caution you for obstruction.'

Joe put the book down. 'Just out of curiosity, did the Duchess say anything about your suggestion? Did she dismiss it out of hand or...?'

'Not exactly. She was concerned how it might look, so it must have crossed her mind. She did say that she's not very comfortable around him, so maybe there is something in it.'

'Not feeling comfortable around someone is not a reason to suspect them of murder,' Harnby said dismissively. I looked up at her.

'Don't shout at me, but I was wondering...'

Harnby was taking a drink of her strong black coffee and I watched one of her eyebrows rise into an impressively high arch. It was rather comic, but now wasn't the time to laugh.

'Well, stop wondering,' she said after swallowing. 'Put that on your list of things to stop doing. Stop wondering. Joe, do me a favour, grab me one of those chocolate brownies.' She handed him a five-pound note. 'Leave that on the side.'

'You know you don't have to...'

'Pay? Yes, I do. Okay, while he's gone, what are you wondering? If it's something I can clear up for you, then I want to stop your cogs turning and help you put all this to bed, but I can't be seen setting him a bad example.'

'On the night of the murder, Arianna and Miranda were seen arguing. Did you find out what they were arguing about?'

'Is that all you want to know? Okay, well, they were arguing about posters. Can you believe it? Posters. Miranda felt the Festival press office hadn't been giving *Romeo and Juliet* enough attention, that it should have featured more prominently in the Festival's promotion campaign. That was it, nothing more scandalous than that, I'm afraid.'

'I presume Arianna told you that?'

'She did, and before you tell me we only have her word for it, we have a reliable witness, and they had argued about it before in front of the cast. Sorry to disappoint you.'

'Here you are, boss, one chocolate brownie.'

'Thanks, Joe. Right, drink up, we need to get back to the office.'

CHAPTER 21

After a day of highs and lows, I had gone home and tried to distract myself with housework, cleaning my small terraced worker's cottage. I didn't possess a lot of 'stuff', but there was enough to keep me busy for a couple of hours. Pumpkin was fine with the dusting and tidying, but the vacuum cleaner was not a welcome visitor and she hid under the bed until I dragged the beast upstairs, at which point she launched herself over the electric monster and down the stairs with such a bounce, she only touched the carpet once about halfway down. She scurried into the kitchen, where I'd eventually found her perched on top of the fridge.

After cleaning, I had ground enough coffee for the next couple of days, taking pleasure in the aroma that permeated the kitchen as I turned the handle on my antique coffee grinder. I'd put my ironing board away for the first time in months and thrown out the vegetables I'd bought in a moment of health-focused enthusiasm, which in the end had sat in the fridge long enough to go mouldy. Then I'd brought the evening to a close with a long, hot bath.

Pumpkin had ignored me for what remained of the evening

and had spent the last hour or so staring down the gap at the side of the fridge. This told me we had a small furry visitor and at some point I could expect to be presented with a gift, which I would have to feign great surprise and pleasure at. Fortunately, there was no sign of it when I left the house this morning; it was a treat I was going to have to wait for.

After two mugs of strong coffee, I threw myself into helping my team out. I'd neglected them for far too long and DS Harnby's words were starting to sink in. The more I thought about my conversation with the Duchess, the more I realised that I was treading a very fine line. I had received quiet support from the Duke and Duchess over the last couple of years, but I did need to focus on my job, and I did need to be sure of my information before I questioned their decisions. I had to remember that they were fundamentally my employers.

I am very fortunate: I have a job I love in a beautiful building, wonderful friends and a nice home. Perhaps it was time to appreciate what I had and get on with my job. So, that was what I was doing. I kept an eye out for Richard as I worked, but with the exception of Stanley, who made his daily visit for a sausage roll and mug of hot water, I didn't see any of the cast or crew.

Tonight was opening night. The performance would be attended by media from up and down the country. Originally intended to be a local affair, it had gained nationwide attention thanks to Miranda's involvement, but her death meant that journalists were now clamouring for tickets in order to review a production that would go down in history for the wrong reason. Sponsors would attend, along with VIPs, and friends and family of the production members would be amongst the audience. It would be followed by a small party with an outside caterer providing a bar, something I wasn't involved in, so I would be able to attend the performance as a guest.

One thing I had decided to do after the lunchtime rush was make some marchpane as a gift for the cast. Marchpane is referenced in act 1, scene 5 of *Romeo and Juliet* and often created at times of celebration, so it seemed appropriate. An early version of marzipan, it was used to make ornate edible decorations. I used ground almonds, sugar and rose water to make a stiff paste. Once it was dough-like, I rolled it out, then the fun started.

After a couple of hours, I had what was meant to be the tragedy and comedy masks of the theatre. If I'm honest, they looked more like something that children might wear on Halloween in order to terrorise the neighbours, but from the right angle, you could just about work out what I'd intended. With the remaining marchpane, I made a number of little daggers and poison bottles. I used natural food colouring to liven them up a bit, although the choice of yellow giving the impression of gold leaf on the masks made them look like they had a bad case of jaundice. If ever there was a time that I needed people to respond with 'It's the thought that counts', this was it.

'I'M GOING to take the marchpane to the green room, and then head home. I have no idea what I'm going to wear tonight and it'll take at least one gin and tonic and multiple tantrums for me to decide. I should probably just let Pumpkin choose an outfit for me.'

Mark didn't look convinced by that idea. 'Yeah, that'll help you score with Richard, an outfit covered in cat hair and paired with accessories made of furballs and chicken-scented treats. You could get Joyce to help you pick out an outfit, repair your friendship while she chooses your shoes.' As he looked at me wide eyed, I knew he was already picturing the end result. Outwardly, I ignored his comment about Richard, but I was spending a bit more time mentally trawling through my wardrobe than usual.

'Not a chance, I'd like to maintain some sense of dignity. Now, go on, skedaddle, or I'll tell the Duchess you'd like to spend more time in tights and a codpiece.'

'Alright, I'm going.' And with that, he made his exit and I was left wondering what I owned that was clean and still fitted me. There was no way I was asking for Joyce's help. Hell would have to freeze over first.

It was necessary to pass the end of the Wright Room in order to reach the *Romeo and Juliet* company's green room. The space had been closed to visitors since Miranda's murder, but staff had been allowed back in. I paused briefly and glanced down towards the end of the room, shivered and kept going; I really didn't have any desire to linger.

Down a narrow corridor, up a short staircase, round a corner and I was outside the green room. The door was open a crack and I was about to knock having heard voices, especially as I recognised them as coming from Stanley and Damien and I wanted to wish them luck. But I held back; it sounded like they were having a 'deep and meaningful'. There was no laughter or lightness in their voices.

They were only hours away from the first performance with a full audience, so the stress levels must be high amongst the company, that all-important adrenalin coursing through their veins. I had no doubt that they didn't need any distractions, so I placed the marchpane display carefully on a small table that had been left outside the door and put the good luck card I had written for the company next to it. It was impossible to miss and I could be sure the cast would see it as they came in.

The words *'now she's out of the way'* stopped me heading straight back down the stairs. It was Stanley speaking, now back to sounding exactly the same as always: as if he was smiling and could burst into laughter at any moment. But none of that was reflected in his words.

'If you'd told me sooner, I could have dealt with her sooner. You waited far too long to do anything about it.'

'I didn't want Hannah to find out, she still mustn't know. She can't know I lied to her for so long.' Damien sounded miserable.

'She doesn't have to, she won't hear it from me. You were an idiot not to tell her in the first place, but the problem is dealt with now and you can move on. I've always dreamt of the day I'd walk my little girl down the aisle, and now I will. There's no reason to drag your heels anymore – get a ring on the girl's finger and make my Hannah happy.'

The idea of Stanley as father of the bride should have given me a wonderful image of a proud man on one of the happiest days of his life, but that image was being crowded out of my brain as I tried to work out exactly which of them had dealt with 'the problem' and what it was they'd done.

CHAPTER 22

I walked towards the main entrance of the house. Tonight, I was a guest – no taking short cuts through the staff entrance or dashing to the office to finish a piece of work quickly. Joyce, Mark and I had made an agreement that tonight was all about relaxing. We would see the house as the other ticket holders did, immerse ourselves in the story of tragic love and allow ourselves to be transported back to the 1930s.

Large flambeaux torches lit the entrance to Charleton House and the stone glowed a deep yellow in the flames. Strips of light were cast up the Romanesque columns and the shadows danced as the excited chatter of guests spread through the groups. The atmosphere was contagious, and I felt my own excitement grow.

It was only then that I remembered I hadn't been to the theatre since I had moved to Derbyshire from London. It had been far too long and I had no excuse: Manchester, Sheffield and Leeds aren't too far away and all have fantastic theatres, and of course, Richard was going to be working at the Leeds Playhouse for a couple of months, which made it even more appealing.

Joyce was waiting for me by the steps, perfectly positioned next to a torch and looking rather goddess-like, dressed from head to toe in black. A tight-fitting dress that she must have spray-painted on clung in all the right places, and a few of the wrong places, too. It stopped just below her knee, revealing the legs of a twenty-year-old. She had paired the dress with a long, flowing, thin black cardigan that hung open to ensure we didn't miss a thing and created the effect of a dramatic cloak. Her straw-blonde hair was pinned up with curling tendrils hanging at the sides. Her blood-red lipstick added a dramatic flash of colour – it was alluring and terrifying in equal amounts.

Mark walked up beside me. 'Cruella de Vil, you are looking marvellous and extremely... theatrical.'

'Everyone in the theatre, regardless of their job, seems to wear black like it is some kind of uniform, so I thought I would join them and dress appropriately.'

'Well, stay away from garlic and wooden crosses and you'll be fine,' Mark warned.

We walked through the entrance, past the ticket desk closed for the night, along the deeply patterned carpet, past white marble statues of Venus and Cupid, and out through a further set of doors into the cobbled courtyard. Here we were greeted by more torches. Modern uplighters were also discreetly dotted around, throwing light up the walls of the building.

The shadows of dancing partygoers were projected around us and I watched as the black figures moved to the sounds of the jazz music that was being played through hidden speakers. If I stopped and followed their movements, I could see the interaction between some of the figures as they drank from coupe glasses and welcomed one another. The sounds of clinking glass and laughter played over the music, and if I closed my eyes, I really could believe I had just stepped into the swirling mass of a 1930s party in full swing.

Mark looped his arm into mine. 'I've been told we receive a complimentary drink if we head through, so come on, let's get in the spirit of things.'

I allowed him to lead me on. He took the occasional skip in time with the music and I could hear him humming along.

As we waited at the bar, he gave me a good look up and down. 'I must say, that dress looks rather magnificent on you. We're going to have to find more excuses for you to get dolled up.' After hours of choosing outfits, only to toss them aside one after the other, I'd stumbled across an old favourite at the back of my wardrobe: a dark green empire-waist dress with short sleeves that I hadn't worn since I'd lived in London. I'd felt rather self-conscious, but Mark's compliment gave me a warm glow and I relaxed.

Mark had dressed for the setting and was wearing a black double-breasted dinner jacket which had square shoulders and made him look broader than his true skinny frame. He sported a black waistcoat underneath it, but then Mark would have worn a waistcoat whether or not it fitted with the setting of the play. A black bow tie and white pocket square completed the outfit, and his shoes were two-tone black and white brogues. He had waxed and styled his moustache neatly, without its usual dramatic curl, and looked extremely handsome.

With our glasses of wine, we stood under an archway, watching more of the audience arrive and listening to the music. I could see Arianna and Maxwell Mountford talking to the Duke and Duchess. They were both smartly dressed, but hadn't opted to take on any of the 1930s style. Maxwell looked particularly pleased with himself and his barrel chest made him resemble a puffed-up pigeon. Arianna's appointment as the first director at the Charleton House theatre had been announced this afternoon, so he could openly display his brotherly pride, or quite simply gloat, depending on how you wanted to look at it. The Duchess caught my eye as she scanned the crowds, holding my gaze for a moment but giving away nothing of her feelings.

I watched as Joe ambled over. He gave a little wave as he saw us.

'Ellie not with you?' I asked as I kissed him on either cheek.

'She has to work. There's a small team of Conservation staff on tonight, ready to break the arm of anyone who gets within fifty yards of a Botticelli.'

'We don't have a Botticelli,' Mark pointed out.

'Then no one will get their arm broken,' his brother-in-law replied happily. I watched Joe's eyes run the length of my outfit. He smiled and nodded his approval, looking decidedly impressed.

'Hello, my loves.' I hadn't seen Ginger arrive. She scanned her eyes up and down Joyce's outfit. 'Bloody hell, can you breathe in that?'

'I'll breathe when I'm dead,' stated Joyce firmly, before taking in the vision that stood before her and losing all ability to speak. Ginger had been transformed. Her rather solid shape had curves, and her ample bosom had been provided with the scaffolding to sit high and was as likely to catch as many eyes as Joyce's own display. An evening gown of metallic blue, cut on the bias, flowed down her figure. The back was cut low, and as she walked, a little train flicked behind her. A fur wrap covered her shoulders and her hair was now in tidy waves that became big, loose curls at the bottom, the mix of silver and white shimmering.

She reached forward, placed a finger beneath Joyce's chin and pushed it up. 'We'll all fall in if you don't close your trap. Didn't realise I could scrub up quite so well, eh? Like it?' She gave us a twirl. 'Or are you afraid of the competition?'

Normally, Joyce would have had no problem responding with a put down. After all, there was no such thing as competition for her, but she didn't let out so much as a squeak.

'I think she needs a drink.' Ginger looped her arm through Joyce's and dragged her in the direction of the alcohol.

I turned back to Joe. 'Is Harnby coming?'

'Yes, she's here, with a date.'

'Ooooh,' giggled Mark. 'A bit of gossip, that's what we like. Where is he, then? What's her type?'

Joe looked towards the door, an amused look on his face. We watched in silence as Harnby stopped to talk to the Duchess and introduce her to the attractive woman who had arrived with her.

'Well I never.' Mark sounded genuinely surprised. 'Mind you, my gaydar has never worked.'

'GOOD EVENING, it brings me so much pleasure to welcome you to my home on such a lovely evening,' said Richard, or rather Capulet. He was similarly attired to Mark, but his dinner jacket was a burgundy red, the pocket square replaced with a white carnation. His hair seeming greyer, he looked distinguished and appeared a little older.

For the first time, I registered just how handsome he was, as opposed to cute. He wasn't the only cast member circulating; I had already seen Lady Capulet welcome people as they entered, and Tybalt was kissing the hands of a group of attractive young women. Richard gave a formal nod of his head, winked at me and strode towards an elderly couple who had been watching him with interest.

Ginger, who had returned with Joyce after they'd consumed a glass of white wine each, looked distracted. She was watching Damien, who was deep in conversation with a man I recognised as a journalist from a local paper.

'I wonder how long until we hear the happy news?' she mused aloud.

'What happy news?' I asked Ginger.

'The night before Miranda was killed, she told me that she and Damien weren't actually divorced. She had been unable to bring herself to sign the papers, despite Damien's protestations; she always intended to, she just found it so hard. Now, Damien is free to move on and marry Hannah. If that's what they want, of course.'

We all turned to face her.

'Bloody hell, woman, why didn't you tell us this before?' spluttered Joyce.

'I didn't want to sully her reputation any further. There was so much talk about the screaming harridan of a director, it didn't seem right, and it's the kind of thing the police would have easily discovered, so they didn't need to hear it from me. She was going to sign and get everything sorted as soon as the play was up and running.'

I looked over at Mark, who shrugged. 'Damien has an alibi.'

'Yeah, provided by his girlfriend, the only other person to be directly affected by Miranda's actions.' But as soon as I said it, I knew that wasn't quite true. I thought back to the conversation I'd overheard between Damien and Stanley – so this must have been the crucial information Damien hadn't shared with Hannah. But that meant there was one other person who was keen to see Miranda loosen her hold over the couple.

I thought back to what Stanley had said: *'If you'd told me sooner, I could have dealt with her sooner.'* It wasn't clear whether he had acted, but would have done so earlier, or whether he would have acted if he'd known. I tried to pick his words apart, feeling sure that the sweet man who had made me laugh every morning wasn't capable of hurting a soul, but I couldn't focus. The volume of the music had increased and the actors had disappeared into the crowd. Crew members in long black t-shirts were directing us to return our glasses and head into the house.

It was time for the play to start.

CHAPTER 23

It was astounding just how different the house felt. Despite spending my working days walking through the rooms and corridors, I seemed to have been transported into an entirely different place and time. Watching the cast perform in their 1930s costumes, I felt as though I was watching the ancestors of the Duke as they lived through a period of love, hate and, ultimately, tragedy. It was easy to imagine that the portraits on the walls were Capulets or Montagues, not Fitzwilliam-Scotts.

The dresses of chiffon and silk, all cut on the bias with elegant flowing lines, their hems nearly touching the floor, were beautiful and showed off the glamour and wealth of the families the actors wearing them were portraying. We followed the action from room to room, back out into the courtyards, and eventually returning inside. The play had been cut in length, but I was still grateful when I was able to find a window ledge to perch on, or a bench to sit on and rest my feet as I enjoyed the action. At one point, Joyce removed her shoes entirely; it seemed she found spending so much time standing hard work as well.

Damien had managed to perform wonders with the lighting; he didn't just illuminate the rooms, but the atmosphere and moods of the characters were enhanced with deepening shadows, or warm glowing candlelight. From time to time, there would be a moment of stillness in a scene and it would appear as if we were looking at a tableau. Damien had created paintings.

Although there wasn't much that could be altered in the rooms, he had also added objects: a discarded jacket here, empty teacups there, a servant bustling through, a bed that had been left unmade – little things that helped turn the Capulets and Montagues into the residents of Charleton House. By the end, I felt like it would take a long time for the shadows of these new inhabitants to leave the rooms.

Seeing Damien's subtle, clever touch everywhere I looked actually made it difficult for me to really enjoy the evening as I wrestled with his talent and the motive he had for Miranda's murder. Each time Stanley appeared dressed as Friar Laurence, the kind friend to Romeo and Juliet determined to see true love win out and bring peace to Verona, an internal battle commenced within my mind. And then there was Lady Capulet, Hannah, unaware of what had been going on around her.

From time to time, I found myself standing close to Maxwell and Arianna Mountford, who were able to relax and enjoy the production in the knowledge that it was Miranda's last. By the time the play ended and the cast took their bows to rapturous applause, I was exhausted and dizzy with names, faces, alibis and motives. I didn't know whether I needed a coffee, a gin and tonic or a very long sleep.

WE MADE our way back down to the courtyard where the bar had been set up. It was unusually warm and we wanted to make the most of our surroundings whilst not actually having to work. It was quite a novelty to be served drinks instead of serving them, not having to worry about whether my staff had turned up on time, or whose turn it was for a break.

Not everyone stayed for the party and the crowd had thinned out a little. Cast members gradually appeared, after they had changed into modern dresses and casual suits, and threw their arms around friends and family, before saying hello to journalists and having their photograph taken.

'Very clever masks, Sophie, thank you. I hadn't actually eaten marchpane before tonight, despite being the one who mentions it in the play,' said the young man playing Peter, a Capulet servant, as he made his way to the bar.

'Thank you for emailing the recipe, Sophie,' called Arianna. I nodded politely.

'I don't want to stay too late, it's been quite a taxing week.'

I looked at Joyce, pretending I didn't recognise the woman who had come out with such an uncharacteristic statement.

'Don't tell me you're full of energy?'

'Actually, no,' I replied. 'I'm dead on my feet. But I would like to see Richard, say congratulations.'

'Of course you would. Well, off you go. I want to track down Ginger. I still can't believe how she looks; I might have misjudged her on the fashion stakes.'

'She worried about the competition?' Mark appeared beside me having heard Joyce's final comment.

'I wouldn't go that far. I don't know anyone who could genuinely compete with that man-eater, but Ginger did go through a bit of a transformation.'

'Ready for another drink?'

'No, I'm good. I was going to try and find Richard.'

'And abandon me, thanks. I've not seen him come down yet and I believe a couple of them were sharing a bottle of champagne upstairs before they joined the fray. Why don't you go up? I'm sure they wouldn't mind, and I saw Ginger head that way. I'm going to find Harnby and get an introduction to her girlfriend.'

I gave him a quick kiss on the cheek and walked across the courtyard, glancing up at the row of gilt-edged windows on the top floor. This must have been where the cast stood to wait for one another on the night of the murder as I could see someone in one of the windows, just as Richard had been.

I stopped and took a step back; the figure in the window didn't look familiar. They were formally dressed, but I didn't recognise them as part of the cast. Then I realised who I was looking at and immediately felt sick.

I took a deep breath and picked up my pace across the courtyard, bits of conversation coming back to me. I needed to talk to Ginger.

CHAPTER 24

'Sophie, join us for a drink.' Stanley held his glass in the air. He was sitting on a windowsill, talking to the woman who'd played the nurse. They were both rosy-cheeked and looked as though they were well on their way to finishing a bottle between them.

'Thanks, Stanley, but I'm looking for Ginger. Has she come this way?'

'She has indeed.' He grinned. 'She was looking for Richard, who I'm sure you'll be happy to see, too.'

'Thanks, and well done. I loved it.'

'Cheers, love, be sure to come and join us for a drink later.'

Now I was certain that Stanley hadn't killed Miranda, I could relax around him and my congratulations were heartfelt. I guessed that in his earlier conversation with Damien, he had been referring to doing no more than talking to Miranda, attempting to convince her to finalise the divorce. He hadn't been talking about killing her.

I retraced the path I had taken many times over the last couple of weeks as I headed away from the company green room. Again, I would pass the entrance to the Wright Room, and again I would be reminded of Miranda lying on the floor with the rope around her neck. This time, the door was closed, and despite it being made from thick wood, there was no mistaking the sound of Ginger's voice coming from the other side.

I didn't bother to knock; I knew who Ginger was talking to, even though I had yet to hear his voice. Richard turned towards me as I stepped into the room.

'Sophie, I was going to come and find you. Ginger and I had just finished.'

'It didn't sound like that to me. It sounded more like Ginger was getting into her stride, and I'd really like to hear what she has to say.'

He looked momentarily confused before a smile slowly reappeared on his face. 'Ah, Miss Marple has been at work.'

Ginger's face was set hard, but as she spoke to me, there was understanding and relief in her voice.

'The window?' she asked. I nodded.

'Yes, the window. Amongst other things. What's that?'

Ginger held a newspaper clipping that Richard tried to snatch from her, but she avoided his grasp and brought it over to me.

'Dammit,' Richard mumbled.

It had been cut from a local newspaper dated twenty-nine years ago. A large group of fresh-faced smiling students beamed out from the photo; a young Miranda, who looked considerably more self-assured than the others, was standing to one side. The article spoke of the upcoming school production of *A Midsummer Night's Dream*. I scanned the happy faces with their broad, confident smiles. I looked at each face in turn while Richard and Ginger waited expectantly.

'No rush,' Richard said, sarcastically. It stung to hear him talk to me that way, but then I reminded myself that the fact I couldn't find him in the photo was important and simply matched everything else I'd started to line up in my mind. I looked at him. His eyes – which seemed to have turned from hazel to mud brown and lost their shine – locked with mine, daring me to say out loud what I knew to be true.

'You started the fire,' I said, certain in my conclusions. So certain that any affection I'd had for him was swept away. 'You've always claimed that you were near the school theatre because you were in rehearsals, but you're not here in the photo. You weren't in the play. Why hasn't anyone picked up on that?'

'I never said anything about being in the play, not until recently. I thought that claiming to have some theatrical links to the area would create a little more press interest. No one was going to remember I wasn't in the damn play; not even Miranda queried it until the night she died, and she directed the thing. It was almost thirty years ago. I can't remember the boys who were on the school cricket team with me, not all of them, and she couldn't remember everyone who was in the play.'

'She started to question it before then, though, didn't she?' said Ginger. 'It was Miranda who found that clipping amongst everything I'd saved from around the time of Leo's death.'

I felt momentarily dizzy as it hit home that Richard had also killed Ginger's brother; that was a part of this I had briefly forgotten. I tried to refocus and go through everything else that made me so certain of Richard's guilt.

'Miranda was asking about tattoos and scars in the pub, not because she was thinking of covering up a scar of her own, but because she guessed your tattoo was hiding something. I'm also guessing that you didn't return to school not because the other college had a drama class, but because of what you'd done, and the large burn you'd gained in the process that's now hidden under the ink on your arm.'

'And Daddy was the head teacher,' Ginger added. 'Are you close to your parents? I don't think so. Miranda told me you haven't spoken to them in years. I'm guessing your father knew what you'd done and got you a last-minute place at the college to keep you away from the school instead of turning you in, especially when he realised that this meant you'd probably started the fire at the village hall, too. He protected you, and then wanted nothing to do with you, not once you were old enough to leave home.'

I could see that each time she spoke, Ginger took a deep breath. She was doing a remarkable job of holding it together in front of the man who had killed her brother.

There was a loud thud as the door behind me flew open and swung back. I cringed as I thought about the possible damage it had just done to the wall behind it. Detective Sergeant Harnby stood in the doorway, closely followed by Joyce who had her shoes in her hand.

'Joyce was worried, she hadn't seen you both in a while,' said Harnby suspiciously as she looked between the three of us. My guess was that Joyce was more likely to be annoyed at being abandoned than worried, but I could understand why someone who didn't know her well would come to that conclusion. 'Would someone like to fill me in on what's happening here?'

I allowed Ginger to explain Richard's role in Leo's death. Richard remained expressionless until he suddenly bolted for the door at the far end of the room. He reached for the door handle, but stumbled backwards as it opened and both Joe and Mark stood on the other side. As Richard took a couple of steps back and attempted to steady himself, he rested his hand on the top of one of the brass posts that held the thick green rope replacing the red one, removed following its use as a murder weapon. He was standing exactly where I'd found Miranda's body, looking at me with hard eyes.

'I'm guessing that in one of her directorial rages, she told you what she had worked out and you reacted by killing her.'

'You'll have a hard time proving all of this – most of the cast have told you I was in the green room when Miranda was killed.' He stood up straight, confident of himself, his charming smile back on his face.

'Ah yes, the window.' Ginger smiled at me.

'Can someone tell me what's going on?' Harnby sounded annoyed, so I put her out of her misery.

'Depending on where you stand in the courtyard, you can see clearly into the window of the green room. There are a number of portraits on the walls. When the cast looked up on the night of Miranda's murder, they did see someone in the window, only it wasn't Richard; it was the portrait on the back wall. It's not a very wide room so the portrait isn't that far away from the window. It's a male, with dark hair, looking down at some papers and from a distance you could be forgiven for thinking it's Richard. Close up it looks nothing like him so no one would have picked up on it.'

Realisation spread across Mark's face and he spoke with an element of surprise in his voice.

'So as a matter of fact, your fellow cast members actually provided an alibi for the Earl of Crowborough. Not that I'm convinced he needs one, he's been dead for 100 years.'

'Why didn't we realise this sooner?' Harnby asked. I explained.

'We've had such good weather recently, and when it's really bright, the sun reflects on the windows and creates a mirror effect. You look at the window and all you can see is the blue sky. At night, on the other hand, when it's dark and the light is on in the room, you can see the portrait. None of us have been in the courtyard at night, and if the cast members have been leaving after evening rehearsals, then they just haven't been standing in the exact same spot to experience the illusion again. Did you know about that, or was it simply good luck?' Richard smirked.

'I guess I'm a very lucky man.'

Ginger walked towards Harnby and the door behind her, making a final comment.

'So while the cast were providing an alibi for a 19th-century aristocrat, Richard, on the other hand, was in here, where he'd killed Miranda after she'd confronted him over the death of my brother.' She seemed to have come to the end of what she could cope with. She passed Harnby and Joyce and left the room. Joyce, with a look of concern I didn't see very often, turned and followed her. I handed Harnby the newspaper clipping and walked out too.

CHAPTER 25

'I couldn't warm to him. I suppose he was reasonably good-looking, I just didn't think he was an appropriate match.'

Joyce was explaining why she'd always felt that Richard wasn't good enough for me.

'I have particularly high standards for anyone who wishes to date our Sophie, and I just didn't feel he was up to par. I'm sure there is someone out there who will gain my approval, but it certainly wasn't going to be Richard Culver. I had no clue he was a killer, though.' I was impressed and moved. That was the closest Joyce had ever come to expressing any kind of affection for me, and I doubted I'd hear anything like it again for some time.

I had brought an extra-large cake out of the fridge and placed it in the centre of the table before handing out forks to everyone. We had settled in the Library Café; only the wall lights were on and it made the room feel a little bit like it was bathed in the glow of candles. Mark had somehow managed to lay his hands on a couple of bottles of the wine that was being poured at the start of the evening. I was glad we didn't have to pay for it; it was pedestrian at best and I made a note of the name to ensure I never ordered any for our cafés.

There was a scrum of hands as everyone grabbed a fork and tucked into the cake. I hadn't bothered to bring out plates; I figured no one would mind just diving in. It felt like the kind of evening that suited tackling an entire uncut cake.

'So then, Soph,' said Mark through a gooey mouthful, 'who *did* you think had killed Miranda? I assume you're not so desperate for a man that you would have continued having romantic chats over coffee with Richard if you'd suspected him.'

'No, I'm not that desperate, thank you very much. I wasn't sure for a long time, and then when I learnt about Miranda not signing the divorce papers, I decided that was key to this. I was worried it could have been Stanley when I overheard him and Damien talking, but then I remembered that when she was killed, Stanley had believed that Damien and Miranda were actually divorced. So then I wondered if Hannah had found out what Damien was trying to hide from her, and Stanley had provided an alibi for her.'

'How did Richard escape your attention?' After a stern look from Joyce following his first question, Mark had at least waited until he had an empty mouth before speaking this time. I sighed.

'I was attracted to him, I admit it.' Joyce raised her eyes to the ceiling at my rather obvious statement. 'As soon as I heard he had an alibi, I immediately discounted him. I would never have wanted to view him as guilty, so I believed everything he said and didn't question what I heard from the others, either. Not until I noticed the illusion in the green room window and found Ginger, who showed me that newspaper clipping.'

'Well, you got there in the end,' Mark said, sounding impressed.

'No, I didn't. I can't take credit for this one at all, and I'll be making sure Harnby and Joe know that.'

I looked across at Ginger, who was quietly demolishing a

large section of the cake. The loose curls having fallen out and formed barely noticeable waves, her hair was starting to look like its old, less glamorous self. The fur wrap had been tossed onto another table and both she and Joyce had kicked off their shoes.

'Had you been trying to figure out who had started the fire all this time?' I asked her.

'On and off. It depended how I felt, but when I saw that Miranda was comin' to the area, I thought it might give me the chance to find out more. I did all I could to increase the chances of her staying with me so I could try and find out what she remembered.'

'But when I went into your house, I couldn't see any photos of Leo. Had you hidden them from her?'

'In the beginning. I didn't want her to work out who I was straight away; I wanted to build up her trust, so I hid them. One night, after a few drinks, the truth came out. The more we talked, the more she remembered things, and she started to put two and two together. I told her not to say anything to Richard until we were sure, but it seems her temper got the better of her. She must have told him what she suspected during a row and he killed her to stop her talking. But she can't have told him that I was involved, or I reckon he'd 'ave come after me.'

'Why didn't you report what you knew after Miranda's murder?' Harnby asked. She and Joe had walked in as Ginger had been explaining.

'Because he had an alibi. I was hoping I could find out something more about his role in the fire, something that he couldn't argue with. I was even going to talk to his parents, see if I could convince them to come forward with what they suspected. But then I saw the same thing as Sophie earlier tonight. I saw the portrait through the window, and that changed everything. I couldn't hold back anymore.'

'Has he confessed?' I asked Harnby.

'Not outright, but thanks to Ginger's work, we can start

piecing everything together and I have no doubt we'll be able to charge him.'

'Why did Richard start the fires in the first place?' Joyce asked. I glanced up at Harnby.

'I'll interrupt if I disagree,' she said to me.

'I assume the fire at the village hall was teenage stupidity. I doubt he meant to burn the place down. When it came to the fire at the school, I imagine it was a combination of frustration at not being chosen for the play, the challenge of being the son of a headmaster – he said himself he didn't get on well with his father – and that he actually got a bit of a kick out of setting the village hall on fire and wanted to do it again.'

'Was he a budding arsonist?' Mark asked Harnby. She shook her head.

'I doubt it was quite that bad. There are plenty of incidents where teenagers have accidentally burnt buildings to the ground simply because they started a fire in a skip nearby or were sitting under a wooden porch playing with matches. My guess is that he was just a troublesome teenager who made a couple of rather serious mistakes, rather than someone who had a career as an arsonist ahead of him. The close proximity of the headmaster's house to the school grounds no doubt meant he was a familiar figure in the vicinity, helping remove him as a suspect. I'd need to check the files, but it might be that no one saw him at the school at all. He also might not have had any idea that there was anyone still in the theatre, or not bothered to check, and that's probably haunted him for years.

'Now then, we want to take statements from each of you before you leave.'

'Can't we do it tomorrow?' Mark implored. 'It's been a long night. You could come round for a beer, Joe.'

Harnby looked horrified. 'It's not a social call. No, we cannot do it tomorrow. I want as much of this wrapped up as possible tonight.'

'I was just thinking of you and your date.' Mark smiled mischievously. 'You could continue your evening with her, and then talk to us tomorrow. We're not leaving the country.'

'That's very considerate, but it's not happening. In fact, I think we'll interview you last. I'm sure you can keep yourself busy. Ginger, would you mind coming with us, and then you can get off home?'

Ginger smiled gratefully and put her shoes back on. As she walked past, Joyce reached for her hand and gave it a squeeze.

'Has any of that cake not been mauled by you lot?' queried Joe. 'Cut me a slice, will you, Sophie?'

'Me too,' said Harnby. 'What is it, anyway?'

'Chocolate mashed potato cake.' I looked over at Mark and his face fell, a forkful of cake hovering outside his mouth. He paused before shrugging.

'It's not bad. Very moist.'

After Ginger had left, I turned to Joyce.

'She'll be alright.'

'I know that, she's a tough old girl.'

'Just like your sister?'

'Exactly like my sister.'

'You'll keep in touch with her, then?'

'Are you kidding? We're already planning a holiday together, and a couple of weekend breaks.' She smiled. 'I feel like I've got a bit of Bunny back. I'm not daft; they're quite different in some ways, but Ginger's got the same spark, and she speaks her mind. Doesn't let me get away with anything, either.'

There was a pause before Joyce looked at me again.

'You will find him, you know.'

'Who?'

'Whichever fella you're meant to be with.'

I thought for a second, and then laughed.

'I'm really in no rush, and besides which, I have all the men I need in my life right now.'

We both looked across at Mark. He had a glass of wine in one hand, a forkful of cake in the other, and a lump of chocolate frosting attached to his moustache. He grinned, oblivious to our conversation.

'What?'

'I was just thinking what a catch you are.' He smiled at me and raised his glass. We laughed before Joyce grabbed the plate and pulled it to our side of the table.

'Give that here, I've got some catching up to do.'

MURDER FOLLOWS Sophie and her friends to London in ***A Capital Crime***. Sign up for Kate's newsletter at www.katepadams.com to find out when ***A Capital Crime*** is available to buy.

I HOPE YOU ENJOYED THIS BOOK

I really hope you enjoyed reading this book as much as I did writing it. I would love you more than I love coffee, gin and chocolate brownies if you could go on to Amazon and leave a review right this very moment. Even if it's just a one sentence comment, your words make a massive difference.

Amazon reviews are a huge boost to independently published authors like me who don't have big publishing houses to spread the word for us. The more reviews, the more likely it is that this book will be discovered by other readers.

Thank you so much.

READ A FREE CHARLETON HOUSE MYSTERY

Building a relationship with my readers is one of the best things about writing. I occasionally send newsletters with details on new releases, special offers, interviews and articles relating to The Charleton House Mysteries.

Sign up to my mailing list and you'll also receive the very first Charleton House Mystery, *A Stately Murder*.

Head to my website for your free copy and find out what happens when Sophie stumbles across the victim of the first murder Charleton House has ever known.

www.katepadams.com

ABOUT THE AUTHOR

After 25 years working in some of England's finest buildings, Kate P. Adams has turned to murder.

Kate grew up in Derbyshire, the setting for the Charleton House Mysteries, and went on to work in theatres around the country, the Natural History Museum - London, the University of Oxford and Hampton Court Palace. Every day she explored darkened corridors and rooms full of history behind doors the public never get to enter. Kate spent years in these beautiful buildings listening to fantastic tales, wondering where the bodies were hidden, and hoping that she'd run into a ghost or two.

Kate has an unhealthy obsession with finding the perfect cup of coffee, enjoys a gin and tonic, and is managed by Pumpkin, a domineering tabby cat who is a little on the large side. Now that she lives in the USA, writing the Charleton House Mysteries allows Kate to go home to be her beloved Derbyshire everyday, in her head at least.

ACKNOWLEDGEMENTS

Thank you to my beta readers Joanna Hancox, Lynne McCormack, Helen McNally, Eileen Minchin and Rosanna Summers. Your honesty and insightful comments help make my books so much better than they would otherwise be.

Many thanks to my advance readers, your support and feedback means a great deal to me. Thank you to all my readers. I love hearing from you.

I'm extremely grateful to Richard Mason, my police advisor who guides me on procedure and makes sure I am, largely, within the law. When I break the rules, that's all me!

My wonderful editor Alison Jack, and Julia Gibbs, my eagle-eyed proofreader. Both are worth their weight in gold.

Thank you to my wife Sue, who encourages me to continue along this path.

Printed in Great Britain
by Amazon